# Paper Chase

**A Detective Ryan Chase Thriller, Volume 3**

M K Farrar

Published by Warwick House Press, 2022.

# Chapter One

"Thank you for coming," Tova Lane called out across the studio audience, "and goodnight."

She opened her arms, and the thunder of clapping and whooping filled her ears. Beaming, she lifted her hand in a wave. People got to their feet, continuing their applause.

"And that's a cut," the director shouted.

Tova glanced back over her shoulder to where the anxious woman she'd been interviewing still sat on her stool onstage. Tova gave Anna Farnham a smile and nod of encouragement and mouthed 'you did great' at her. One of the runners approached Anna and led her off set.

Filming had ended, so Tova stepped down from the stage to greet people and sign autographs. She was fully aware that she was no one without her fans. The moment people stopped wanting to watch her, her career would be finished, and the thought terrified her. Who would she be without her work?

The audience was ninety percent women, but there was a scattering of men among them. Most had been dragged along by their wives or girlfriends, but a few were there alone. It did make her uncomfortable, especially when they used their larger presence to push to the front of crowds and demand her attention. At only five feet one, she couldn't pretend she didn't sometimes feel vulnerable.

One such man was doing exactly that now, calling her name, drowning out everyone else.

"Tova! Tova, over here!"

If she ignored them, they got angry. If she paid extra attention to them, she worried they'd get the wrong idea. She wasn't a man-hater, but experience had left her wary.

She took the photograph of herself that the man held out and scribbled her autograph across the front. She flashed him a smile—so as not to either look like she was too standoffish or too friendly—and handed it back to him, quickly turning to the next person who wanted her autograph.

"Thanks, Tova," the man called. "I'm your biggest fan."

She gave him that smile again, polite but reserved.

"Time's up, Tova," the director said.

Relief soaked through her. "Sorry, everyone. That's all I can do for today. Thank you all for coming. I hope to see you again."

A collective groan rose from those she hadn't managed to get to, but she couldn't sign autographs for hundreds of people in one go—she'd be there all night. Besides, her work wasn't quite done. She needed to check up on Anna Farnham, who the show had centred around that afternoon.

She left offstage. Members of the crew rushed up to her, congratulating her on the successful show. She thanked them each in turn, but her focus was on locating her guest.

She found Anna backstage. The woman's face lit up when she spotted Tova approaching.

"How do you think it went?" Anna asked.

"You did great. I promise."

Anna bit on her lower lip, and her fingers knotted in front of her body. "I don't know. I talked too much, didn't I? I kept rambling on."

"You were fine, I promise. You came across as sincere and honest, and that's really important. The viewers will believe in you."

"I hope so. Over the past couple of years, it hasn't felt as though many people have."

"Tides are changing, Anna. That's why we wanted to make this show. It's important that people who've been through what you have speak out so that if other women find themselves in your position, they can feel confident enough to come forward, too."

Tova reached across the space between them and squeezed Anna's hand.

Anna nodded and sniffed. "You're completely right. That's why I did it. I didn't want anyone else to feel like they didn't have a voice."

The topic of the show had been on the 'me too.' movement, specifically looking at abuse in the workplace. As a solicitor, Anna had been working in a 'men's club' environment, where she was constantly treated with nothing but disrespect by the male partners. It had started with things that could be considered mere irritations such as being ordered to make coffees for them all during important meetings, or her ideas never listened to or taken into account, but things had soon escalated. As months passed, she'd put up with lewd comments and 'accidental' brush-ups in the lifts or corridors. She'd been desperate for the job so had kept quiet, but they'd taken her silence as acceptance. Everything had culminated during a work team-building night away, when the men had all been drinking heavily and moved from lewd comments and brush-ups to full-on groping. They'd pinned her up against a wall and touched her breasts, making out as though they were playing a game where each of them could guess what size bra she wore. She'd managed to get away from them and left the hotel and went to the police to report the abuse. Unfortunately, even when the police went to have a 'talk' with them, they'd all claimed she'd been drinking, too, and had been egging them on, enjoying herself, when a sudden bout of guilt made her turn on them. There hadn't been any CCTV in the part of the hotel where it had taken place, and no outside witnesses had come forward. It was just her word against theirs, and there were more of them than there was of her.

Anna never went back to that job and had a hard time finding a new one. The partners spread the word among their peers that she was a troublemaker and, before long, her name was tainted. It wasn't until she'd responded to a call out from Tova's production team that others in the industry came out to say they'd experienced something similar—not only with that particular firm but in the industry as a whole.

"Remember what we told you about staying off social media after the show releases," Tova told her. "You've been very brave doing this under your own name, but like we warned you before, there will be backlash. Internet trolls are everywhere, and they love jumping on topics like this. Nothing triggers pathetic, rejected men like a woman standing up for herself. They will track you down on social media and do what they can to drag you to their level."

"I've shut all my accounts," Anna said. "There's nothing for them to find."

"That's good, but I'm sure you still have an email address and a phone number. Just be aware that some trolls will get hold of those, too."

Anna paled.

One of the set's runners, who was only just out of university, most probably after completing a degree in media or something similar, approached nervously. "Sorry, Ms Lane, but the studio is booked up for the next hour." It was his way of telling her they needed to leave.

"Yes, of course. We were just going."

Tova walked Anna to the staff exit, but Anna paused before leaving. Tova could tell there was something the other woman wanted to say.

"Umm, can I call you if I do get one of those trolling things?" she asked.

Tova's stomach sank. She hoped Anna hadn't got the wrong idea. Yes, she'd asked lots of questions about the things Anna had been through and had shown genuine sympathy, but that didn't make them friends.

"Honestly, it's probably best if you call the police if you receive something that concerns you. They're better qualified to deal with things like that than me."

She felt like a total bitch for saying it, but she couldn't be a personal support for everyone she interviewed.

Anna's cheeks flared with high red spots. "I'm sorry, that was a stupid thing to ask. I mean, you're a celeb and everything, and I'm basically no one."

Tova wasn't exactly a celebrity. Yes, she got recognised on the odd occasion when she was out in the city, but that was only because she was local and also happened to be working for BBC Bristol. She'd told Anna not to read her social media, but she needed to follow that advice herself. However, it was in her contract that she used social media to promote what she was working on. She had to post a certain number of times per day to Instagram and Twitter and Facebook, and now the younger crowd were coming in with Snapchat and TikTok and God only knew what else or where it would stop. Sometimes she felt as though she was living more of her life online than anywhere else.

"Don't be silly." She touched Anna's arm. "My production team will be in contact to let you know when the piece will air. Take care of yourself, okay?"

"I will and thank you."

Tova waited until Anna had walked away. She let out a breath and walked back to her dressing room. She gathered up her coat, picked her car keys out of her bag, and then caught the lift down to the car park situated beneath the building. The car park was for employees only, so at least she didn't need to worry about bumping into Anna again.

Instantly, she was hit with a fresh pang of guilt, but she couldn't take on the emotions of everyone's stories or she would drown under them. In her job, she had to keep a certain level of detachment in order to not only interview from an unbiased perspective, but also so she didn't take everyone's pain and grief home with her. She wished she could tell people's happier stories, but other than the occasional two-minute cute special about how a lost dog returned after a year, or some kid was camping in his garden to raise money for charity, those weren't the things that got people tuning in. As much as the viewers would have denied it, they wanted to hear about all the terrible things that happened to people in the world—just so long as they happened to *other* people and not them. It made them feel better about their own lives, that yes, maybe they were in a boring marriage, or worked a job they hated, or couldn't afford the credit card bills each month, but at least they weren't being abused or homeless or any number of other social issues that Tova reported on.

She had her head down as she strode across the car park, fishing once more for her car keys. She'd had them in her hand a moment ago, but she must have dropped them back into her bag. Or had she put them in her pocket—

Tova glanced up, just to make sure she'd also remembered where she'd parked her car that morning, and ground to a halt. Her jaw dropped open.

"What the fuck?"

Sprayed across the paintwork of her silver Audi TT were the words: *Who's next?*

Tova's heart all but crawled in her throat. She didn't want to take another single step towards her vehicle. There was something menacing about the words. Strangely, she felt as though they knew something about her that she didn't understand.

Had this been done by someone she'd interviewed?

She looked over her shoulder, suddenly sure she'd find someone behind her—perhaps with a spray cannister in one hand and a bloodied knife in the other, but the space was empty.

Was the person responsible for the graffiti gone now? Surely they wouldn't have hung around, waiting to get caught. The only reason she could think of for staying would be because they meant to harm her. The thought sent chills running through her.

Footsteps came behind her, and she spun around, her heart hammering against the inside of her ribcage, her mouth running dry.

Her director, Emmett Callan, approached her, a frown of concern on his face. He was in his forties and was tall and handsome, in an overly groomed kind of way. He had only recently returned to work after the loss of his partner.

"Tova. Is everything okay?"

"No, it's not." She couldn't imagine Emmett would be much help against a madman with a knife, but she still felt better having him here. "Look at what someone has done to my car."

His eyebrows shot up. "That's terrible. Who would do such a thing?"

Tova blew out a breath. "I have no idea."

"It's a weird thing to write as well, isn't it? Do you know what it means?"

She shook her head. "Maybe it wasn't meant for me." She grasped at straws, trying to make herself feel better. "Maybe whoever did it got the wrong car."

"Possibly, but look, there are security cameras at the entrance to the car park. If the person responsible came that way, they might have been caught on camera."

That was a point. Where the hell were security? Wasn't it their job to stop shit like this happening to their cars?

Was this the work of one of those women-hating scumbags who she'd been warning Anna Farnham about? They filmed in front of a live audience, but the show itself wasn't broadcast live, except for when they did specials. If this was the work of someone who'd seen it, it would have to be a member of their studio audience, and she'd take a good guess that it was most likely one of the male members. She could probably find out the names of those sold tickets, but it wasn't as though she'd be able to throw accusations at people without having any proof.

"You should report this to the police," Emmett said.

"Oh, I fully intend to, but first I want to talk to security. Were they even working today?"

Righteous anger took over her fear. She preferred that emotion. It made her feel strong instead of weak, and one thing she hated was weakness. She stormed through the car park to the booth at the entrance where one of the security guards sat with his head bent. Was he asleep? No wonder her car had been vandalised if the bloody security guard slept on the job.

"Hey!" She banged on the glass, and he jerked upright. She'd been wrong about him being asleep—he'd been looking at his phone.

He cleared his throat. "Ms Lane. What can I do for you?"

"What can you do for me? You can explain why someone vandalised my car while you were busy watching your phone."

His chubby cheeks flushed crimson. "Someone's damaged your car?"

"Yes, and you'd know that if you had been doing your job right."

He got to his feet and stepped out of the booth. "Show me."

Tova marched back to her car and gestured at the graffiti. "Look at that."

His eyes widened. "When did that happen?"

"I'm going to assume some time between me parking it this morning and about ten minutes ago."

He shook his head. "No, I did my rounds an hour ago. I would have spotted the graffiti if it had been on the car then."

She put her hands on her hips. "Good, then that means we have a narrow window where it happened which should make it easier for the police to track down who did this."

"Do you want to call the police?" He seemed surprised.

Her frustration was building by the minute. "Of course I do!"

"They won't do anything. They'll just give you a crime reference number for your insurers, but they won't actually investigate anything. They've got more important crimes to be dealing with."

"This is important!"

"I'm sure it is," the security guard said, though she could tell he was just trying to placate her. "I'm just telling you what the police will say."

She dragged her hand through her blonde hair. "Fine. I'll phone them when I get home."

Emmett, who'd been watching the conversation, put his hand on her arm. "Are you going to be okay getting home?"

"Yes, Emmett. It's the outside of the car that's been damaged, not the engine, I'll be fine."

His lips tightened. "That's good 'cause I have plans anyway."

She was aware she was sniping at someone who was only trying to help, and she deflated. Her director had been having a rough time himself lately, and he didn't deserve her shortness.

"Sorry," she said. "I'll be fine. I promise."

"Will you text me when you get home, just to let me know you're safe."

"I will." She turned her attention to the guard. "At the very least, I expect you to go through the security cameras, see if there's anything unusual that I can report to the police."

He took out his phone again to check the time. "I'm about to knock off for the day act—"

Her glare cut him off.

"I'll see what I can do," he muttered.

"Thank you."

She was going to have to drive through the city and park outside her building with that on the side of her car. She read the words again. *Who's next?*

A shudder ran through her.

# Chapter Two

D I Ryan Chase from the Major Crimes Investigation Team of the Avon and Somerset Police kept his face schooled in an expression of calm so as not to portray his horror at the scene before him. He'd seen plenty of dead bodies in his time, but he wasn't sure he'd ever seen anything this graphic.

The body of the young man lay splayed out in a pool of blood on the concrete floor of the warehouse. He'd been cut open from sternum to groin, and much of what should have been contained within layers of skin and muscle and fat were now spilled in sausage-like, bloodied coils.

"Looks like a wild animal attack," Ryan's sergeant, Mallory Lawson, said from beside him

Ryan shook his head. He doubted there was much more than the occasional fox or dog around these parts. "No animal was responsible for this. This could only have been done at the hands of another human."

It was late, and Ryan technically wasn't on duty at this time, but control knew to alert him out of hours. It wasn't as though he slept much anyway, and he preferred to focus his mind on work rather than lying in bed, staring at the ceiling, fighting his own thoughts. He did feel slightly guilty at dragging Mallory out as well. Mallory had the responsibility of her brother at home—though Ollie was an adult, he had Down's Syndrome, and a recent accident had made him nervous to be alone, especially at night—but her parents had been at the house, so she'd insisted it was fine.

The road outside the warehouse had been sealed off with an outer cordon, response vehicles and uniformed officers blocking the way. It was gone midnight, and they were on the outskirts of Bristol, surrounded by fields. The nearest built-up area of Whitchurch described itself as a village rather than part of the city. They weren't likely to get too much foot traffic or even passing cars, either at this location or this time of night, but all precautions to conserve the scene and any potential evidence needed to be taken.

The huge warehouse dwarfed the team of uniformed police, Scenes of Crime Officers, and detectives inside. Pigeon shit covered everything, the birds responsible perched on metal beams above, watching the scene below. Cracked, dirty glass filled the windows positioned high in the walls—too high to allow anyone to peep in from outside, but low enough for the blue pulse of the emergency lights to filter in. Large portable floodlights had been set up inside so the team could see what they were doing. Other than the team of police and the body, the warehouse was almost empty. A vast space that contained only items that had been fly-tipped in a couple of the corners—an old mattress and some bulging black bin bags.

"DI Chase."

Ryan turned at the male voice.

Manny Perin was the sergeant in charge of coordinating the scene. He was young—in his thirties—with an olive skin tone and jet-black hair and dark eyes.

"This looks pretty brutal," Ryan said as Perin approached. "What have we got?"

"Victim is male, Caucasian, in his late twenties, early thirties, at a guess. His body was still warm when he was found, so he's not been dead long."

"Where are we with finding out the victim's ID?"

"Nothing on the body—no wallet in his pockets or anything like that. It's going to be a case of checking recent misper files against his description and running fingerprints, DNA, and dental files."

"Any sign of the murder weapon?" Ryan asked.

"Not yet, but we have SOCO going over the scene and we're going to need to pull in some search teams for the local area as well. It's possible whoever did this tossed it as they made their escape."

"You're thinking a knife?"

Perin nodded. "From this injury, I'd say so, and a sharp one at that."

Ryan crouched and studied the giant wound running vertically down the victim's torso. Blood soaked the victim's shirt, which had been torn open to give access to the body. Buttons were missing—cut off, perhaps, or popped off when the shirt had been undone.

Ryan glanced around on the floor. "Have you spotted any buttons?"

It would give them an idea if the victim had been moved to this spot from somewhere else, or if he'd been taken straight there.

"There's one over here," Mallory said, pointing down. "And another one here." She gestured for one of the SOCOs to come over to mark them.

"So we know his shirt was torn open here then."

Ryan studied the rest of the victim's clothing. One of his trainers was missing. "What about the other one? Any sign of that yet?"

"Not that we've found," Perin said, "but we've only just started the search."

Ryan's keen mind noticed something. "Do you see how the bottom of his sock is clean? If he'd been made to walk here with a missing trainer, it would be dirty. The floor is covered in pigeon crap."

Mallory nodded. "You're right. You think someone carried him in here?"

Ryan arched his brow. "I can't imagine he hopped."

She appeared to be suppressing a laugh. "That would mean he was either already dead or unconscious when he was brought here."

"Exactly. Let's hope he remained unconscious when this was done to him. There's a lot of blood, which points towards him still being alive, but there would be if the cut was made close to death and livor mortis hadn't set in yet."

Normally, he'd be able to take the amount of blood present at the scene to give him an idea if the victim's heart had been beating at the time of the stabbing, or if they'd bled out elsewhere and been moved, but it was unclear here. He couldn't see any obvious defensive wounds either. The post-mortem would give them more detail, but any initial clues he could take from the scene would help. Time was of the essence when it came to tracking down a killer.

"The cut seems deliberate," Ryan said. "One stab wound cut downward, rather than the multiple stabs of a frenzied attack."

Sergeant Perin nodded. "I agree. This has been done with a sharp knife, possibly even a scalpel."

"They'd have needed to have the stomach for it." He winced. "No pun intended. Any signs of vomit nearby?" It could be a possible way to get the attacker's DNA if they'd lost their guts midway through the killing.

Perin straightened. "We haven't found anything yet, but that doesn't mean it isn't around."

"Or the killer just had a strong gut." He realised he'd made another pun. "Sorry."

Ryan studied the area around the body and then lifted his head to take in the rest of the warehouse. "Why choose this place? What connection does the killer have to this warehouse? How did they know it would be empty and free from CCTV? They must have been here before to be aware of those things. Whoever did this must have planned it. It wasn't spontaneous. We need to find out how long it's been empty for and what it was used for before that."

Mallory took out her phone and typed out some notes for herself. "I'll check into it, boss."

He took a moment to consider the scene. There weren't any other buildings overlooking the warehouse and, in the time they'd been here, hardly any other traffic had gone past. He was aware of a garden centre about a mile away, and there was a spattering of properties within the same sort of distance before the fields turned into the village.

"We're going to need to track down whatever CCTV we can—whatever is nearest."

Perin nodded. "I've got a couple of uniformed officers seeing if any of the nearby property owners saw or heard anything unusual. They're asking about possible CCTV as well."

"Do we have any ANPR cameras nearby?"

The sergeant shook his head. "Not this far out. There's one on the Bath Road, but I'm not sure how much use that is going to be to us."

"Who found the body?" Ryan asked him.

"Bunch of teenagers who'd come up here to hang out—and by hang out, I mean drink and get into trouble."

"Who was the first to spot the body?"

"Sixteen-year-old Cameron James. The others weren't far behind him. He was also the one to call triple nine."

"Where are they now?" Ryan asked.

"I got one of my officers to take them down to the station where we called their parents. It's late, and I couldn't just let them go straight home, not after seeing that." He gestured at the body.

"I'll talk to them there then," Ryan said. "Find out if they saw or heard anything. If this is a regular hangout spot for them, they might have noticed someone lurking around over the past week or even longer. Our perp might have been checking the place out some time before the actual murder took place. There's also the chance they might have even disturbed the killer. Though what kind of motive someone would have to want to do something like this, I can't even imagine."

"This could be some kind of warning to someone else?" Mallory suggested. "Perhaps even gang-related?"

"It's possible. Until we know more about the victim and what kind of thing he's been involved in, it's pure speculation at this point. Finding out who he is needs to be one of our top priorities. If we know who he is and what his final moments were, it'll go a long way to narrowing down who might have done this to him."

# Chapter Three

I t was hard not to have the image of the victim with his guts spilled out burned onto his brain. Ryan hoped the man was dead before someone decided to open him up.

They drove back into the city. It was quieter now, the early morning hours belonging to night shift workers and those out partying. It meant traffic was light, and it didn't take them more than twenty minutes to make it back to the station.

The parents had been called and were all waiting with the teens in reception. It was easy to pick them out among the drunks and sex workers by the way they were all together, around the same age, expressions of worry and frustration at being called out in the middle of the night.

The witnesses would need to be separated and taken to interview rooms. It was important that they didn't influence each other or change their stories to match that of their friends'.

The parents spotted Ryan and Mallory walk in.

One of the women, in her late forties, hurried up to them. "Excuse me, can you tell us what's going on? Are the kids going to be traumatised by this? I want to know if my daughter is going to wake up screaming every night for the next however many days or weeks."

She acted as though Ryan was the one who'd allowed their kids to hang out in an abandoned warehouse and who had deliberately placed a body for them to find.

Ryan wanted to tell her that they were police officers, not psychiatrists, but he held his tongue, not wishing to antagonise her.

"In my experience, teenagers are pretty resilient, but I can put you in touch with a Family Liaison Officer to talk through any worries you might be having. For the time being, however, we are going to need to talk to each of the children individually, and they will need an adult present."

The witnesses consisted of two boys and two girls, all sixteen years old. Since it was late and they were on a skeleton staff, Ryan had already decided he would interview Cameron James, the boy who had been first to come across the body, and Mallory and a couple of his detective constables could interview the others.

"Cameron James?" he called out.

"Over here."

Cameron was a lanky boy with light-brown hair cut in a style that was supposed to be fashionable, but to Ryan just looked messy. He already wore a bored expression, his knees on his elbows as he stared at his phone. His mother sat beside him, chewing her lower lip, her face pale with anxiety.

"Would you like to come through?" he said. "I'll try not to keep you too long. I know it's late."

He led them through into one of the interview rooms. Ryan gestured for them both to sit.

"Hello, Cameron. I'm DI Chase. I need to ask you some questions about what happened tonight, to find out what you may have seen or heard. I'm going to record our conversation so I can refer back to it later."

The boy was slumped in his seat, his arms folded, a sulky look on his face. "Am I in trouble cause of the booze?"

Ryan shook his head. "No. A bit of underage drinking isn't our concern right now."

"I didn't know he was drinking," his mother said tightly. "I thought he was at his friend's house."

"Which friend is that?"

She shot her son a look of disapproval. "Jayden. He was with them all tonight, too."

"I know you must be upset that he lied, but I doubt he'll want to go back to the warehouse anytime soon."

Once the shock had worn off, he could well want to go back—they all might. It would turn into a kind of Halloween night dare, to return to the site of the crime. Ryan didn't believe they had anything to do with the death of the young man, but they couldn't completely rule it out. They wouldn't be the first teenagers to kill and they wouldn't be the last. But they didn't have any blood on them, and whoever had done that to the victim would have been covered. Maybe they'd got changed? But without a car, they'd have had to have hidden bloodied clothing somewhere around the area, and if they had, the search teams would find it.

The most obvious answer was normally the correct one, and right now the story the teenagers had given them was the most likely.

Ryan went through the formalities, taking down their names and Cameron's date of birth and address.

"Cameron, I'd like you to talk me through the events that led up to tonight."

The boy didn't meet his eye. "What do you mean?"

"Well, you told your mother you were staying at a friend's house, but you ended up at an abandoned warehouse instead. So, what time did you leave home?"

"About seven."

"And you didn't go to Jayden's house?"

"Yeah, I did." He shuffled in his seat, his feet scraping the floor beneath the table. "And then we left his and met the girls."

"What time was that?"

"About eight. I think."

Ryan jotted it down in his notebook. "So why did you decide to go to the warehouse?

He shrugged. "Just somewhere to hang out."

"The warehouse is pretty far out. How did you get there?"

"We walked."

"How long did that take?"

He shrugged. "Dunno. Half an hour or so."

"You reported finding the body at ten-thirty, but you went out about eight. What were you doing between leaving the house and going to the warehouse?"

That shrug again. "Just hanging out."

"I need more details than that. You're going to have to give me times and places."

Cameron's gaze flicked towards his mother.

"It's okay, Cameron," Ryan assured him. "You're not going to get in any trouble.

The boy sighed and rolled his eyes. "Fine. We were hanging around outside the Co-op in Whitchurch, trying to get someone to buy us alcohol."

"Right. And if we check the CCTV footage at the shop, that's what we'll find?" Ryan doubted they'd need to do that, but it wouldn't do the teenager any harm to understand that they could track his movements, if needed.

"Yeah, you will."

Ryan moved on. "What time did you arrive at the warehouse?"

"A few minutes before I called nine-nine-nine."

"So, about ten twenty-seven?"

"Yeah, I suppose."

"When you approached the warehouse, were you coming from the main road or a different direction?"

"From the road."

"Were there any cars around?"

He shook his head. "No, I don't think so."

Ryan sat back. "I want you to think, Cameron. Any detail could be important at this point, no matter how small. Did you see any people around? Or was there anything that caught your attention?"

He twisted his lips as he thought. "The warehouse door was open. I thought that was strange. It's normally shut, and we have to pry it open ourselves.

"It's a place you go to often then?"

"A couple of times a month maybe."

"And have you ever seen anyone else hanging around?"

His brow furrowed. "There was a car a couple of weeks ago. It sped off as we arrived. I worried it was police at first, but then I thought they wouldn't have just driven off, they'd have stayed and asked what we were doing there."

"Can you remember what make of car it was, or did you manage to see any of the number plate?"

"Nah, sorry. I didn't really think about anything like that. It was dark, though. Maybe black or grey. And it was a posh one, too. New and like something a businessman might drive."

"What time would it have been?"

"I think about eight. Yeah, just after eight."

The car might belong to the killer, or they could just have been someone there for a completely different reason.

Cameron slumped lower. "Can I get out of here now? It's late and I'm knackered."

"We won't be too much longer, Cameron."

He sighed dramatically. "This is bullshit. I already told you I didn't see nothing."

Ryan had come across plenty of teenagers like him before. Simultaneously thought the world was against him and that it owed him everything. He hoped it was just a phase the boy and he wouldn't carry the bad attitude through to adulthood. Ryan didn't want to be sitting across an interview desk from him in a few years to come, interviewing him as a suspect to a crime rather than just a witness.

"I have to ask you these questions, Cameron. It's my job. A man was brutally murdered, and even if you don't think you saw anything, you might have inadvertently come across something that could help us. Maybe it was something you *didn't* see that will give us a clue as to who did this."

Cameron's eyes narrowed. "I don't even understand what that means."

Ryan tried not to sigh. "Never mind. Back to the car. Can you be more specific about what day you saw it?"

They might be able to catch the vehicle on a traffic camera somewhere nearby and get a number plate from it. It was a long shot, but it was worth taking.

"It was two weeks ago, on Friday night."

"And what direction did it go in? Towards the city or away?"

"Towards the city, I think."

He'd have to see if any of the other teens remembered seeing this car. One of them might have a better recollection of it. If they could get a make or model, or even a partial plate, it would help narrow things down.

"I'm sorry for keeping you," he nodded at his mother, "you, too, Mrs James. If anything else comes up, we may have to call you back in for a follow-up interview, but I'm hoping we've covered everything. My colleague can give you the details of the Family Liaison Officer. They'll be in touch to see if you need any support."

"Thank you, Detective." Mrs James flashed him a tired smile.

Cameron jerked his chin in a nod of acknowledgement but didn't meet Ryan's eye.

Ryan ended the recording and got to his feet. He thanked them both again and saw them out of the building.

It was getting late—or was it even considered early now? He'd do a full briefing in the morning. SOCO might be finished at the site by then and have something more for him. He needed to get his head down for a few hours.

Tomorrow was going to be another long day.

# Chapter Four

Macie Ostrow opened the pill box for the correct day and stared down at the assortment of tablets in various shapes and colours. The thought of swallowing them all once again already made her throat close over. She had to fight her gag reflex every time, tears forming as she tried to choke them down. It wasn't as though she had a choice. These weren't vitamins.

She needed to take the medication to stop her body rejecting the donated heart, but she wished she didn't have to. A part of her had believed that once she'd got the transplant it would be a whole new her, that she wouldn't feel like she was sick anymore, but things hadn't quite gone that way. She had a new fear now—fear that the organ would fail or her body would reject it. The heart wouldn't last forever, and then she'd be back in that awful place of waiting and praying.

Before she'd fallen ill, she'd lived an exciting and adventurous life. She'd backpacked to places like Thailand and Bali, but ultimately that had been her downfall. On her last trip, she'd come down with a virus that had left her with cardiomyopathy—chronic heart disease.

Macie placed the first of the pills on the back of her tongue and took a large swig from the glass of water on her nightstand. Thankfully, it went down, and she took the next one.

Downstairs, the sound of her parents moving around the house drifted up to her. She was twenty-seven years old and still living at home. It was another source of her depression. She should have a life by now—her own home, a job, a boyfriend, and maybe even thinking about starting a family—but she couldn't see that ever happening. She couldn't envisage a life for herself that wasn't governed by her illness.

No, she was supposed to be well now, everyone kept telling her so.

She placed her fingers to the large, twisted red scar that ran down her sternum to the base of her ribs. At only three months post-surgery, it was still healing and looked hideous. She'd never wear a low-cut top or, God forbid, a bikini or swimsuit. She wouldn't be able to stand the people staring at her with questions in their eyes.

Her therapist told her she should own the scar, be proud of it, because it meant she was a survivor, but Macie didn't feel that way. In her eyes, she had something inside her that another person had had to die to give her, and that made her a kind of monster. A Frankenstein's monster.

Macie picked up her phone from her bedside table and then left her bedroom and made her way downstairs.

Her mother was already in the kitchen, making tea and toast.

"Morning, love. How did you sleep?"

"Fine, I guess."

She hadn't. She'd stayed awake for hours, thinking about this alien organ inside her chest, wondering if she could tell that it wasn't meant to be a part of her. Did it beat louder than her old heart had? Did her chest feel fuller? Did she feel like she had a different person living inside her?

She'd lain there as her pain had built, and her pulse had grown quicker.

She should tell all of this to her therapist, but she couldn't bring herself to do it. It felt so fucking ungrateful.

"Good. What have you got planned for today?"

"Some more job hunting."

Her mother offered her a smile. "You know you don't need to rush into anything. It's still really early days since your surgery. Try not to stress about it."

"I'm approaching thirty, Mum, and who knows how many years I have left. I want to have a life."

Her mother tutted, but there was affection in the sound. "You're nowhere near thirty, but I do understand you wanting your independence."

Macie sighed and dropped into the kitchen chair, tossing her phone onto the table. "It's not easy trying to find work when everyone wants experience and you basically have none."

"That's not true."

"Mum, the last time I worked a proper job, I was twenty-four. And I hate having to explain to everyone the reason behind me having a huge gap in my CV. They get all sympathetic and awkward, and I can see in their eyes that they're just assuming I'm going to get ill again at some point and the company is going to have to pay for it. Why would they employ me when they could have someone who is healthy?"

"You are much better now, darling, and a company would be lucky to have you working for them."

Macie snorted. "Do you really believe that? What do I have to offer?"

Her mother's jaw tightened. "Well, if you have that attitude and you refuse to even believe in yourself, how do you expect someone else to take a chance on you?"

Macie knew she was feeling sorry for herself. She needed to figure out how to drag herself out of it. She'd been given such an incredible gift—she could be dead right now—and she was wasting it.

Her mother handed her a cup of tea and slid a plate containing a piece of toast slathered with strawberry jam in front of her.

Macie sighed and sat back. "I'm sorry, Mum. You're right. I have talents."

"You do. You're a whizz on a computer."

"Everyone my age is good at computers, Mum."

Since getting sick, she hadn't had much of a life outside of her online one. Online, she could control what she fed to others. Even while she was posting to Instagram and TikTok details about her surgeries and the things she was going through, she was able to sugarcoat it and only show them the parts that were tolerable for human consumption. She made it look like she was strong and empowered, when deep down, she was falling apart. There had been times where she'd felt vulnerable where she'd posted how she'd really felt, and her views and comments had skyrocketed. But ultimately, she'd taken those posts down, unable to handle the amount of exposure it had brought her. Perhaps she should have embraced those posts, but even though most of the comments were supportive and positive, there were always those trolls who'd comment things like 'you'd be better off dead', and those were the words that got stuck in her head and that she lay awake at night, turning over and over.

"Why don't you think about volunteering somewhere?" her mother suggested.

Macie took a bite of the jam on toast. "It feels like giving up."

"It's experience, sweetheart. That's a good thing. It's not giving up."

"If I'm volunteering somewhere, how am I going to have time to apply for real jobs? And how will I find the time to interview? Plus, it would mean letting someone down eventually, and I'll worry about doing that."

Her mother's tone softened. "You're overthinking it."

"Maybe."

"There are plenty of charity shops that would love to have some help."

Macie pulled a face. She wasn't a fan of charity shops. She wasn't someone who went into them to browse and find some amazing bargain. They smelled weird, and the jumble of various items made it impossible to focus.

"There must be something else I can do other than that."

Her mother laughed. "I'm sure there will be."

Macie's phone buzzed, and she picked it up. She had an email. Swiping her thumb across the screen, she opened it and quickly read through.

"Oh my God. I have an interview!"

Her mother's face brightened. "That's amazing. When?"

"Later today, if I can make it, they said. There's a number I can call."

"What's it an interview for?"

"Nothing exciting. Just answering phones."

"Like a receptionist?"

Macie shook her head. "No, it's a call centre. Like I said, nothing exciting, but it would get me started."

"Just as long as it's not too stressful."

Macie rolled her eyes. "Mum, how stressful can answering phones be? It's not as though I'm applying to be a fireman, or do air traffic control, or be a surgeon. I'll be sitting down most of the time, so it's not physical either."

"I'm sure you'll be great."

Macie gave a tight smile and looked back down at her phone. Those negative thoughts threatened to creep back in again. They were like little black worms burying into her brain. When these thoughts invaded her head, she found herself sinking back into depression. There were times when she found herself sitting in her car, unable to even start the engine, just staring at the steering wheel. She'd be lost in her thoughts as minutes turned to hours and she discovered she'd wasted half the day sitting there.

She beat herself up at how ungrateful she was. The heart should have gone to someone else who would live their lives to the fullest now they'd been given a second chance. That's what she imagined the person who'd donated the organ would have wanted. They'd have pictured their gift going to someone who would do everything they could to make the most of their time and not spend it staring at nothing in their car for hours on end or moaning about taking their meds every day.

Was it survivors' guilt that she was experiencing? She should probably talk it over with her counsellor, but she was too ashamed to admit how she felt. It hurt that someone had died in order for her to live, and she didn't feel that she deserved it.

# Chapter Five

Ryan managed to get a couple of hours' sleep before he had to be back in the office. After downing a large coffee, he called a briefing for his team. They'd all had a late finish and an early start, and he looked around at bleary eyes.

"I appreciate you're all putting the hours in right now, but we need all hands on deck for this one. We have an unidentified young man brutally murdered, and his body left in a disused warehouse just outside of Whitchurch."

The evidence board behind him contained a map, the location of the warehouse marked on it. Together with the map were photographs taken from the scene. They weren't for the faint of heart.

Ryan continued. "We estimate the man to be in in his late twenties to early thirties. He's Caucasian, with light-brown hair and blue eyes, approximately six feet tall and of average build. There was no ID on the body. Is that because he left home without his wallet, or did the killer take it as a memento? We've run his prints, and he doesn't have any kind of record. The victim was wearing jeans and a white shirt that had been torn open in order to inflict the injury seen here." He pointed back to a photograph of the victim. "He was also found to be missing one of his trainers, and it hasn't yet been located. The bottom of the sock of the foot that's missing the trainer is clean, which makes me think the victim was either dead or unconscious when he was brought to the warehouse."

Ryan paused to take in his team, who were either making notes or listening intently.

"If we don't get anywhere with missing persons or a DNA match, we'll start to circulate a photograph of the victim and try a social media campaign. Finding out who he is will be paramount in figuring out who could have done this."

His team nodded in agreement.

"No murder weapon was found at the scene, but we still have search teams working the area." He gestured at the map. "As you can see, most of the building is surrounded by fields with the one road running past it. If the killer dumped the weapon, it could be anywhere around here.

"We have to consider how both the killer and the victim got to this location. I'm not ruling out them walking, after all, that's what the teenagers who found the body did, but the missing trainer makes me doubt that. If the victim came here willingly to meet their killer, there might have been a struggle at the warehouse, and the shoe was kicked off then, but then what happened to it? Since we haven't located it, either the killer took it with them or the trainer was lost elsewhere. If it was lost elsewhere, we know the victim didn't walk there because of how clean the sock was, so the killer, or killers, must have brought him to this location, and I highly doubt they carried the victim all the way out there."

Finding a vehicle would make their job easier. They were more likely to have caught it on a local camera somewhere.

"Tying in with that is the question about whether the victim was already dead when he was taken to the warehouse.

I'm hoping to get a report soon from forensics about blood spatters and possible drag marks that will give us a better idea. As you already know, a group of teenagers found the body. One of the teens I questioned, Cameron James, says he saw a dark-coloured car leaving the area on the evening of Friday, February nineteenth. Dev," he said, focusing on one of his constables, DC Kharral, "can you see what cameras we had in the area on that night, see if you can narrow down some vehicles that we can follow up on?"

"Absolutely, boss."

"Our main focus needs to be getting an ID on our victim. Shonda, I want you on misper cases. If he only went missing late last night, he might not be missed yet, but at some point, someone will notice he's gone and call it in. I want to be one of the first to hear if we get any matches. Got it?"

DC Shonda Dawson nodded. "Got it."

"The location of the warehouse is a good mile outside of the nearest village, so the chance of anyone having seen anything is greatly reduced, but there are some homes scattered around that vicinity, and there's also a nearby garden centre that may have CCTV cameras. We've had uniform going door to door, but that needs to be followed up. Linda," he said to DC Quinn, "I'm putting you in charge of that."

Linda Quinn jotted something down in her notebook. "On it."

He turned to his remaining constable, Craig Penn. "I want the owner of the warehouse tracked down and questioned. Find out who had access to the building and then talk to them. It doesn't look as though it's been in use for some time, but there still might be maintenance that needs doing, or maybe it was being used for storage up until very recently. I think whoever did this already knew the warehouse was empty, so they'd been there before. Perhaps they'd seen it simply by driving past and checking it out, but they might have a closer connection."

"What are we up to, boss?" Mallory asked him from the front row. Her legs were crossed, and she bounced the top foot up and down.

"Let's head down to speak to the pathologist, see if there's anything about the victim that we might be able to use."

She nodded. "Sounds good."

"Okay, everyone," he said, addressing the room. "Let's get moving and make some progress today."

The space became a flurry of movement as his team gathered their belongings and left. Only Mallory remained behind.

Ryan suddenly remembered something.

The timing of this case wasn't great. Donna had her final checkup with the hospital today, and he'd wanted to be there with her. The consultant was going to let her know if the surgery and chemotherapy had done what it was supposed to so that she was now clear from cancer, or else he'd tell her that it hadn't worked. He had a sick kind of dread in his gut at the possibility the cancer might have got worse. The chemotherapy had really taken its toll on her, so it wasn't as though he could look at her and see she'd got better. She was pale and too thin, and she wasn't eating nearly enough and was cold all the time. In Ryan's mind, she was still a very sick woman, and he couldn't imagine the doctors telling her she was well again.

The alternative terrified him, though. Even though he and Donna had been separated for some time now, she was probably still his best friend. He didn't want to lose her.

Right now, though, he wasn't sure he was going to make it to her appointment. This case was disturbing, and he had zero leads. He didn't even know the name of their victim. He wasn't sure he'd get away with going incommunicado for an hour or more while he went to Donna's appointment.

He took his phone from the inside pocket of his jacket and quickly typed out a text.

*I'm sorry but a work thing has come up. I won't make it today.*

It was one of the bugbears of their marriage, that he'd always prioritised work above everything else, and now he felt like he was doing the same thing again. He reminded himself that they weren't married anymore, and he was allowed to put his work first, but it still didn't feel right.

His phone buzzed almost instantly with a reply: *Don't worry. Jen can come with me.*

He put the phone back into his pocket. Donna did have support other than him. One of her friends going with her was fine. He had to work. He shouldn't feel bad about it.

Then why did he have such a heavy sensation in his chest?

Mallory must have noticed his expression.

"Everything okay, boss?"

"Yeah...no, not really. Donna has an appointment at the hospital today. I was supposed to be taking her. She'll find out if she got the all-clear or not."

"So, go. I'll cover for you," Mallory said. "We'd only be going together anyway. I'll just go on my own. I can handle this, you know I can."

He did know she could. She was a good detective and a strong woman to boot. He still wanted to support her as well, though.

"No, it's fine, really. I'll come with you."

"Okay, just let me grab my stuff."

He used the bathroom before he left the office and went to wait for Mallory out by the car. He checked his phone again, in case there were any new messages from Donna, perhaps saying her friend couldn't make it after all. He didn't want Donna to have to go through this alone. But there was nothing.

Mallory came trotting out of the building, pulling her jacket tighter around her body. They'd seen the first signs of spring over the past couple of weeks, but winter hadn't quite let go of its grip on the weather just yet.

"Ready?" she asked him.

"Yeah, I guess so." But still, he didn't get in the car, choosing to remain by the driver's door instead.

Mallory opened the passenger side and paused, looking at him over the roof. "You're having second thoughts, aren't you?"

"Sorry. It's fine."

"Donna needs you more than I do right now," she told him. "Just go."

"What about the victim? He needs me to be on my game, too."

"And you won't be if you're distracted because you're worrying about Donna."

He checked his watch. "I think I'm too late now anyway. She said she was asking her friend to take her."

"Then you'll be there in time to help her through the fallout, whatever that might be."

She was right. "Okay, I'll be back as soon as I can."
"I'll let you know if there's any developments."
"Thanks, Mallory."

# Chapter Six

Tova turned into the underground car park beneath the studio but had to pull to a halt, the barrier guarding the way. Normally, some kind of scanning mechanism recognised her number plate, and the barrier went up automatically, but because she was in a different vehicle, it didn't budge.

She'd had to take her Audi TT to the garage first thing that morning to have the graffiti removed. She was in a hire car now—a decidedly less flashing Honda Civic. She'd thought she wouldn't like driving a hire car, but to her surprise, she enjoyed the anonymity.

The graffiti had thrown her more than she'd first thought. She wanted to convince herself that it hadn't been meant for her, but the fact was, if it had been intended for her, whoever had sprayed that on her car knew which one was hers and where she parked it. They knew when she'd be in work as well. It had set her on edge, and she'd discovered herself driving home with both hands tight around the steering wheel and her jaw clamped shut, every muscle in her body rigid with tension.

As her colleague had suspected, the police hadn't been interested. They'd given her a crime reference number for her insurance and sent her on her way. It meant she was going to have to take this into her own hands.

The barrier still refused to rise, so she honked her horn to get the attention of the security guard instead.

It was the same one as yesterday.

He approached her car and leaned down to her window. "Hello, Ms Lane. New car?"

"I could hardly drive the graffitied one around, could I?"

"No, I suppose not."

"Have you had a chance to check out the security cameras from yesterday?"

"I only just started my shift, and the one yesterday ended shortly after you left."

She exhaled. "That would be a 'no' then?"

"It's a 'not yet.'"

Tova believed she always had to do things herself if she was ever going to get them done properly. It was as though people just didn't care anymore. No one took any pride in their work these days.

"Fine. Well, if you don't have time to do it, send the footage over to me." She reached into her handbag on the passenger seat and fished out her business card. She handed it to him. "My email address is on there. I'll figure out who the hell vandalised my car."

He paled. "I-I don't think I have the authority to do that, Ms Lane."

"You don't have the authority? How about I let your boss know that you were doing your job so badly that you allowed an employee's car to be graffitied right under your nose? I'm sure I don't need to remind you that you were watching your phone rather than the car park."

Was she being a bitch right now? Living up to her minor celebrity status? Sometimes, she couldn't tell if she was being a bitch or if she was just standing up for herself and not letting people walk over her. If she backed down every time someone wanted to palm her off, nothing would get done. Besides, she was a reporter, and that meant asking hard questions and occasionally doing and saying things that made her a little uncomfortable and had her turning those moments over in her head in bed at night. When the day came where she didn't feel bad about those moments, maybe that would be the time when she needed to question her morals. Did telling people they should do better make her a diva? She wished she didn't question herself so much. She came across as a strong, confident woman who knew what she wanted in life, but deep down she worried about what people thought of her.

"Fine, I'll email the footage over," he relented, "but if you find anything, you need to bring it back to me, okay, and then I'll report it back to the boss. You don't mention to anyone that I did this for you, though."

She was aware that she would be doing his job for him, and then he'd take the credit, but she didn't really care. What she wanted was to find out who'd spray-painted her car. The not knowing was what bothered her the most. Had it been someone she knew? Was she going to talk to them today and they'd be smiling at her as though nothing had happened while knowing what they'd done? Was there someone out there who she thought was a friend but who actually thought differently of her?

The wording of the message played on her mind as well. *Who's next?* It was as though whoever wrote the words knew something that she didn't.

"Fine. Can you open the barrier now? I have work to do."

He nodded and went back to the booth. Within seconds, the barrier lifted, and she drove through. Instead of going to the space that was saved for her, she drove to a different part of the car park. No one needed to know the Honda was hers, at least for the day, and if she parked somewhere else, there was no reason anyone would find out.

Tova locked the car behind her and caught the lift up to the studio. Her dressing room also served as her office. The space was windowless and essentially a converted store cupboard, but at least it was hers, and she had her name on the door. She logged on to her computer and pulled up her email, waiting impatiently for the CCTV files to come through. He'd better stick to what he'd promised or there would be hell to pay.

*Ping.*

The email came in. It had a link to the footage in the cloud, together with the login details and the password. She was fairly sure he could get fired for this, but that wasn't her problem. He could easily have offered to do this himself.

Tova blew out a breath and sat back. How far into the footage would she need to go? This was something the police should be doing, but clearly they'd deemed it not important enough for their time. She might be a reporter, but right now she felt like she was playing detective. This was a part of her job, too, though, digging into things.

She'd left her car in the parking spot at eight-thirty yesterday morning, and it was gone five by the time she'd returned. She guessed that meant whoever was responsible for the graffiti could have done it anytime between then. The security guard said he'd done the rounds an hour before she'd returned to her car and hadn't seen anything then, but how much did she trust him? He'd already proven himself to be incompetent. She remembered how he hadn't even glanced up from his phone when she'd approached the security booth—it had taken her banging on the glass to get him to look up. That was hardly reassuring. For all she knew, he was lying about doing the rounds when he had.

There was one way she'd know for sure and that was by watching the footage. If he'd done his job, he'd have been caught on camera.

Tova shook her head. She wasn't watching this to get proof he was bad at his job. She needed it to watch for anyone suspicious hanging around.

The footage was split into six different screens which gave views of various areas of the underground car park. One showed the main entrance, the other the exit. Another showed the doorway leading onto the stairwell that could be taken up to the studio on the ground floor, and the other the set of lifts. Two others were positioned to show the interior of the parking garage, but on none of the shots was her car visible.

"Damn it."

It didn't matter, she decided. Whoever had graffitied her car had to have entered the car park and left again, and she had footage of both entrances and exits. They must have been caught on camera. All she needed was to see someone she didn't recognise, who also happened to be acting shifty—perhaps with a bag that contained the spray can— and she'd have her culprit.

She'd start at the point where she'd discovered the damage and work backwards from there. The paint had been somewhat dry, though still tacky to touch, so it definitely hadn't been done right before she'd arrived, but it also hadn't been done right at the start of the day either or it would have been completely dry. A quick Google search last night had told her that would have taken at least eight hours. At least it gave her a window to work with.

As she hit 'play', her heart sank. There were too many people around. Both vehicles and people entered and exited the car park every ten minutes or so. Some of them she recognised, but most she didn't. That was hardly surprising. The building housed multiple floors of different production companies.

The thing that bothered her the most was that there were so many people around. It wasn't as though whoever graffitied her car had done so in a dark, deserted car park. Okay, maybe the lighting where she'd parked hadn't been great, but why had no one seen them? They must have ducked down between her car and the one parked adjacent to hers and done the spray-painting like that. Would they have got paint on themselves in that position? She didn't know. It wasn't as though she'd ever used a spray can herself.

Tova let out a sigh and put her head in her hands. Unless she spotted someone in a black balaclava and with a spray can in their hand, she wasn't going to be able to figure out who was responsible. She'd have to track down each and every person who'd appeared on camera and interview them herself, and she simply didn't have the time or resources to do such a thing.

She was going to have to let this go. As much as it went against her nature not to keeping digging until she got an answer, she wouldn't be getting paid for this, and she had her actual work to do. Her director wanted a follow-up on one of the stories from last week, and she hadn't got anywhere on it yet, and he was waiting on her.

If she didn't start doing the kind of digging that she was paid for, she wouldn't have a show.

# Chapter Seven

Mallory pulled on the protective outerwear over the top of her grey suit and finished it up with a pair of gloves and wellies. She hoped the post-mortem was going to give them something to go on.

She followed the pathologist into the cool, sterile room. The odour was unpleasant, but not eye-wateringly so. She prided herself on her strong stomach.

The table on the furthest left contained a body, the shape of which was hidden beneath a white sheet.

Pathologist Iain Shepherd was in his fifties, with a thick head of greying hair and a quick smile. She never would have guessed his job if she'd met him out on the street. He reminded her of someone's dad, who liked to tell bad jokes and tease their daughter about boys from school, not someone who spent their days elbow-deep in bloodied corpses and dealing with grief-stricken relatives and disdainful barristers.

"How are you, DS Lawson?" he asked as he led her into the examination room.

"Good, thanks. Busy."

"How about that brother of yours?"

"He's well. Certainly a lot better than this guy." She jerked her chin towards the sheet-covered body lying on one of the metal tables.

"You understand I'm still working on him. I don't have a huge amount for you yet."

"That's fine. We currently have zero leads, so anything you can tell me will help. We don't even know who he is yet. Something as simple as a distinguishing mark might help."

"I'm sure I can tell you more than that."

"Sounds hopeful."

"Wait until you've heard what I've got to say first. It's a curious case, that's for sure."

That piqued her interest. "Oh?"

Iain moved over to the table. "Let's start with the basics." He drew back the sheet, revealing the body below. It was in a better condition than it had been at the warehouse, the organs that had been spilling from the body cavity now fully removed and weighed and bagged, and the blood wiped away. "The victim is a male, Caucasian, approximately twenty-five to thirty-five years of age. He's five feet eleven and eighty-six-point-two kilograms. I believe his cause of death to be blood loss resulting in heart failure." Iain looked over at Mallory. "The cause of the blood loss was a sharp force injury to the abdomen, most likely from a plain-edge knife. Depth of the incision indicates a stab wound, as does the cleanly divided edges. Length of the stab wound is one hundred and thirteen millimetres, which is unusual. I'd say the initial incision was here, at the solar plexus, and then the knife was moved in a downward motion, lengthening the cut.

"Normally in homicides we'd see multiple deep stab wounds, but in this case, there is only this one. I also didn't find any fabric within the wound, which tells me the victim's shirt was opened before the incision was made."

"Was he alive then," Mallory asked, "or already dead?"

"I believe he was still alive at the time of the initial stabbing. However, there are no defensive wounds, either active or passive, on the hands or arms. There is, however, blunt force trauma to the back of the skull, which makes me think that even though the victim was alive, he may well have been unconscious."

She was starting to build a picture of what had happened.

"Jesus. Poor bloke." She didn't want to think about the way the man's guts had been on the outside of his body when they'd found him. She hoped he'd died before the killer had got to that point, or at the very least, had remained unconscious. "How long do you think he'd been dead when he was found?"

"It's not an exact science, but I'd say a matter of hours. The body was still warm, and rigor mortis hadn't set in. With a wound of this size and the exposure of the internal organs to the cold, I'd say he was killed recently for him to still be warm. Taking that into account, together with the lack of rigor mortis, I'd say he was killed somewhere between one to two hours before the body was discovered. I could probably tell in more detail, by measuring the temperature of the liver, but the curious thing is that the patient is missing their liver."

Mallory frowned. "Their liver? A person can't survive without their liver, so I assume it was taken by whoever killed him."

"Yes, I've concluded the same."

"Are we looking at black market organ harvesting?"

"I don't believe so. Surgical removal of the organ would have been required to make that viable, and that isn't what's happened here. Yes, a blade has been used to sever the organ from the body, but it wasn't a careful or precise job."

"Maybe someone was desperate or in a rush?" she suggested. "It could be someone who didn't really know what they were doing and stole the organ, unaware there needed to be a certain method used when it came to actually selling them. Can you tell if the liver was removed before or after the victim had died?"

He shook his head. "I can't tell. The amount of blood loss is so extreme, it could have been caused by the initial section opening up the abdomen rather than the liver being removed."

Mallory hoped it was the first option. The thought of this poor man still conscious with his abdomen cut open and a maniac slashing at his organs would have been a hideous way to go. Their final moments would have been utter horror and agony and terror.

Iain continued. "There's something else, though. I believe this person has had a lot of medical treatment over their lives. Do you see all these?" He pointed to a series of marks running down the inside of the wrists.

Mallory recognised the pattern. "Needle marks? But you're thinking medical treatment rather than drug addict? Why?"

If the victim had been a drug addict, it might give them a motive for why someone had wanted him dead.

"I'd say these were done by a professional. And then there's this." He moved higher up the body to point at a scar on the neck.

"What's that?"

"I believe it's a scar from a transjugular biopsy."

She raised an eyebrow. "A what?"

"It's where a doctor makes an incision on the right side of a patient's neck and then passes a catheter into a neck vein, through the heart, and into a vein that exits the liver. The doctor then inserts a needle through the catheter to get a sample of liver tissue."

"What might that mean?".

"That we're looking at someone who most likely had some kind of liver damage. Unfortunately, the amount of damage that's been caused by the knife wound makes it hard for me to tell what other surgeries they might have had, but considering the liver is missing, it's a pretty good guess. I've sent a blood sample off to toxicology, which I hope will give us a better idea of what's happened."

"Why would someone want to take another person's liver, especially if it was failing?"

He shook his head slowly. "Honestly, I don't know."

Mallory thought hard. "So, our victim might have spent time in hospital?"

"I'd say so. Possibly quite a significant amount of time."

"That's really helpful, thank you. I'll check with the hepatology unit at the hospital, see if anyone recognises him."

"He might not be local," Iain said.

He had a point, but she would get police from all over the country to check with their local hospital departments if that was what it took to find out who their John Doe was.

"Maybe not, but it gives us something solid to go on."

"I'm glad it's been helpful. I'll send over the full report when it's complete."

"Thanks."

Mallory left the building, pulling out her phone as she went. Her first instinct was to call Ryan and give him an update, but then she remembered that he might be in an appointment with his ex-wife, and neither of them would appreciate the interruption, especially if it was bad news.

She prayed it wouldn't be. She'd witnessed Ryan struggle over the past six months. It hadn't escaped her notice how he couldn't leave his desk until all the items on it were perfectly lined up, or how he'd tap his fingers against his thigh a certain number of times and then repeat it until whatever had stalled inside him had righted itself again. Sometimes, he could go for months without any of these habits really showing up, but not recently. Was it purely his ex-wife's illness that had caused the new flare-up, or was it more to do with the man who'd killed Ryan's daughter who'd woken up in the hospital? Perhaps it was both. She couldn't imagine going through what Ryan had. He always encouraged her to start up a relationship and maybe even a family one day, but he didn't realise that whenever he did that, she'd was always thinking that she didn't have it in her to put herself in a position where she might experience such loss.

She decided to get back into the office and update the rest of the team instead. She was their sarge after all. If she could make some inroads into contacting the local hospital and those in the surrounding counties, her boss would have one less thing to worry about.

# Chapter Eight

R yan sat in the waiting room.

Donna had already gone into her appointment by the time he'd arrived. He'd phoned her to see if she wanted him to come into the office with her, but she had her friend with her and said she was fine. He'd considered leaving again, but it seemed a bit pointless now he was here.

He was surrounded by people who were clearly in some form of treatment, their husbands or wives, or friends or parents sitting anxiously by the patients' sides, doing their best to be supportive. He tapped his foot and checked his watch again. This was frustrating. Maybe he should have gone with Mallory instead. He felt like a spare part here and could have been of more use at work. He wondered how his sergeant was getting on. He hoped they'd have some decent leads by the end of the day. Few things were harder than working on a case when the ID of the victim was unknown.

Through the double doors that were propped open, Donna approached, her friend, Jen, close behind.

Ryan rose, his heart lurching. How did she seem? Was she devastated? Was her friend? He couldn't read her expression, and she didn't seem to have noticed him.

Suddenly she drew to a halt and faced the wall. What was she doing?

He hadn't noticed the large gold bell attached the wall until the jangle of it rang through the waiting room. Applause joined the ringing—from both those still in the waiting room and from medical staff who'd gathered around his ex-wife. Donna turned and hugged her friend and then did the same to a couple of nurses. She swiped at her eyes, but from the smile that stretched across her face, Ryan could see they were happy tears.

The bell. Of course, that had a significance, didn't it? It wasn't something he'd ever witnessed before, but he was sure it meant she'd had the all-clear.

Donna must have remembered him, as she turned to the waiting room. People were still clapping, and she raised her hands self-consciously, colour in her cheeks for the first time in what felt like forever. She spotted him, and her smile widened.

A tightness constricted Ryan's throat, and his eyes burned with unshed tears of emotion.

She was okay. She was going to be fine.

"Does that mean what I think it does?" he asked her when he was close enough. Around them, the applause finally died down.

"I got the all-clear. The surgery and chemo worked. I'll have to have regular checkups, but no more chemo."

He pulled her into his arms and gave her a brief but fierce squeeze. "I think that must be the best news I've ever had."

She gave a choked laugh. "Me, too."

"Can I drive you home?" He felt like he should offer to take her out for a celebratory coffee or even lunch—though it was still a bit early—but he was also aware that he was needed back in the office. He shouldn't even be here, really. He was sure

Mallory had a handle on things, but he still felt that internal tug of being needed somewhere else.

"No, I'm fine. Jen is going to take me out."

"Right, of course."

He remembered her friend, and they gave each other a perfunctory nod. This was one of the friends who'd been around when he and Donna had been separating, and he was fairly confident that she wouldn't have heard particularly great things about him over the years. He hoped he'd have made up for it since Donna's diagnosis, but she was only protecting her friend and didn't want him weaselling his way back into Donna's life. Not that he cared too much about what Jen thought of him. Anyway, that wasn't what he'd been doing. Donna had needed some support, and he'd done his best to give that to her. She was better now and wouldn't need him anymore, so she would move on with her life, just as she should.

He was surprised to experience a dip of disappointment at that thought. He was overjoyed that she was well, but perhaps he'd liked being needed again. It was one thing being needed at work—he was used to that—but the intimacy created when you took care of someone you cared about was completely different.

"I'll pop in and check on you tomorrow then?" he said.

She gave him a sympathetic smile, as though she felt sorry for him. "You're always welcome, Ryan, but you don't need to check up on me anymore, remember? I'm better."

He glanced at the floor and scuffed his foot. "I should get back to work then. I'm really happy about your news, Donna."

"Thanks, Ryan, and thanks for everything you've done for me."

He gave a half shrug. "Anytime. I'll see you soon."

He turned and made his way out of the hospital and back to his car, taking his phone out of his pocket. He didn't have any missed calls from Mallory, which he took as a good sign. Or was it? If there had been any new developments with the case, she would have called him, so perhaps that meant the post-mortem hadn't given them anything new to go on.

Ryan unlocked the car and climbed behind the wheel. Before he started the engine, he called his sergeant's number.

"Ryan, hi," she answered. "How did it go with Donna?"

"Good. She got the all-clear."

"That's wonderful news. I'm so pleased for you all."

"Me, too. How did things go with the pathologist?"

"Good. I'll fill you in when you get here, shall I? It'll probably be easier."

He plugged the key into the ignition. "Okay. I'm coming in now. I'll see you shortly."

BY THE TIME HE REACHED the office, his team was already gathered in the briefing room, Mallory standing at the front.

"Ah, the boss is back," she said as he entered. "I was just bringing everyone up to speed."

Ryan waved a hand. "Don't let me stop you."

He took a seat at the back next to DCI Mandy Hirst. She gave him a nod and turned back to the front. Was his boss aware of where he'd been for the past hour or so?

Mallory had places marked out on the map. He wasn't sure what they were at first, but it quickly became apparent once she started talking.

"According to the pathologist, Doctor Iain Shepherd, our victim had been receiving extensive medical treatment. Right now, we're hoping that he's local, but there is the possibility he isn't. The pathologist believes he has a scar that matches an operation called a transjugular liver biopsy which is something that happens when a patient has liver failure. Since the victim's liver is missing, the killer clearly had some kind of interest in the organ, which possibility has to do with the treatment."

Ryan raised a hand to stop her. This was all news to him, and he was just getting his head around it. "You're saying the victim was missing his liver?"

"That's right. Since a person can't survive without a liver, we can assume whoever killed this man was the one to remove it. And since there was no liver found at the scene, we have to assume they took it with them."

Ryan's mind raced. "But it's an unhealthy liver, I mean, if he had to have a biopsy done, I assume it was an unhealthy liver. What would someone do with it? They couldn't sell it on the black market, could they? It wouldn't be worth anything."

"We're unsure yet. The pathologist is running some blood samples, see if he can get a better idea of what stage of liver failure the patient was in."

It didn't make sense. Why would someone steal a damaged liver? What possible use would it be? Unless they didn't know. But what was the likelihood of someone being murdered for their liver and that liver being so damaged the victim had needed a biopsy on it?

Something else occurred to Ryan. "If we're looking at a black-market case here, why just take the liver? Why not take all the organs?"

"Maybe they intended to," DC Dawson called out from her seat, "but they were interrupted?"

Ryan considered it. "They might have heard the teenagers coming."

Mallory interjected. "The pathologist doesn't think we're looking at a black-market situation here. He thinks the cuts that were made were too coarse. The organ would never have been good enough for a transplant, even if it had been healthy."

"Are we looking at some kind of message being sent? Are there any other similar cases we can compare this to?" He toyed again with the possibility of it being gang-related.

"We'll need to check," Mallory said, "but what this information does give us is a way of finding out our victim's ID. Since we haven't been able to find any matches on the misper files yet, we have to assume no one is missing him. If he's someone who's been sick for some time, however, I don't think it'll stay that way. I'd like to think he had someone who would check up on him."

Ryan liked to think that, too, but there were plenty of people out there who had to battle through illness alone.

"In the meantime," she continued, "we can check with the local hospitals and see if anyone recognises him."

"Good work," he told her. He got to his feet and joined her at the front of the room.

She gave him a nod and took her seat again, leaving him leading the meeting.

"How are we getting on with everything else?" he asked. It was still early in the day, but since he had people gathered, he might as well get an update.

"I've tracked down the owner of the warehouse," Craig said. "The place is owned by a shipping company that went bust a couple of months ago. The building is going to be repossessed by the bank."

"Can we get a list of everyone who had access to the building. Let's talk to them all, find out where they all were yesterday evening."

Craig nodded.

"Press are getting word of this," Linda said. "They're coming from all over. The grizzly details are getting out. They're portraying it as some kind of sacrificial murder."

"Jesus." Ryan shook his head. "Who the hell has been talking?"

He liked to think it wasn't one of his people. There were a lot of different teams involved in a case like this, and with police still combing the surrounding countryside, it was bound to get noticed by locals. All it took was one tip-off to the local newspapers and word quickly got round. In fact, these days, they didn't even need a tip-off. They had people scouring sites like Facebook and Twitter for posts that might make a story, so all that would need to happen was for a passing local to take a quick video of all the police and post it to their social media accounts saying something like 'anyone know what's going on in Whitchurch' and the press was bound to jump on it.

"Can you contact our on-call press officer," he asked Linda. "We'll put out a statement about the body or the newspapers are just going to keep speculating. I'm thinking we can use it to our advantage to help us get an ID on this person. Give a description, together with the possibility that he may have been receiving medical care for a liver problem, and someone might recognise the description and come forward."

"I assume we can tell them that we're treating this as a murder investigation?" she asked.

"Yes, they might as well know that, though I hate to think of whoever the victim's family is finding out in such a way. It can't be helped, though. They were going to find out soon enough—assuming he even has any family."

Would it be better if he did or didn't? Ryan was never sure about that answer. Sometimes, he felt like being alone was the easier option. He didn't have to take anyone else into account when he was deciding what to do with his days, but at the same time, it could be unbearably lonely.

# Chapter Nine

Macie parked in the car park of the modern, grey block of a building. A large metal sign told of the insurance company that was located inside—the same company she was here to interview for.

Nerves churned in her stomach, and she swallowed a wave of nausea. Was she sick? No, it was just nerves. She hated going to interviews. Even though this one was just to answer calls and process things on a computer—something that was well within her capability—she felt completely out of her depth. It had been years since she'd worked in any kind of profession—her poor health preventing her from doing so—and she was sure people would take one look at her and know she was different.

There would be all the questions as well, and the main one she dreaded was them asking about the gap in her CV. She'd have no choice but to explain what she'd been through, and there was never any doubt in her mind that their decision to give her a job would be based on that rather than any questions she might have answered previously.

Macie checked the time. She needed to move or she was going to be late, and that was never good. She forced herself out of her little car and straightened her skirt. Her usual outfit of leggings and an oversized t-shirt had been replaced by a white shirt, navy skirt, jacket, and low heels. The shirt was buttoned high to her throat to avoid anyone catching a glimpse of her scar. She hadn't worn makeup for months, but today she'd given her pale lashes a sweep of mascara and applied some tinted balm to her lips. It wasn't much, but she hoped it meant she didn't seem quite so wiped out.

She clocked the sign for the reception and crossed the car park towards it. A couple of smartly dressed men stood outside the building, smoking cigarettes, and they both gave her a nod and a smile as she approached. She returned the gesture, her self-consciousness building with every step, and was grateful to slip through the automatic doors.

Behind the reception desk sat a woman around her age. She was on the phone and lifted a finger to let Macie know she wouldn't be a minute.

Macie glanced around at all the business propaganda on the walls or in the form of pull-up banners, advertising to make this place seem like the best insurance company in the world. It was all bullshit, of course. They'd say that they offered people protection and peace of mind, but actually, all they did was prey off people's insecurities and fears. All insurance companies had done was ensure the pricing of everything had gone up because businesses assumed everyone was insured and so the insurance companies would pay for everything.

Not that she would give voice to her thoughts in the interview. And her moral ideation wasn't strong enough to stop herself receiving a pay cheque from them every month, if they were good enough to offer her a job.

The woman behind reception finally put down the phone. "Hi, welcome to Direct Call. How can I help you?"

"My name is Macie Ostrow. I have an interview at twelve-fifteen with Mr Clark."

"Take a seat." She nodded at the bank of chairs opposite. "I'll let him know you're here."

Macie did as she was told, her handbag containing her CV clutched in her lap. Her heart beat too fast, and being able to feel it only increased her anxiety. She didn't think she'd ever really be able to think of it as *her* heart. It would forever feel like something she had borrowed, or even stolen, and at some point, it would be taken back again.

Her breathing grew shorter, and her palms felt clammy against the fake leather of her handbag. She just wanted to get this over with.

"Miss Ostrow?"

A male voice commandeered her attention, and she looked up to find a man in his fifties in a grey suit staring down at her.

"Oh, yes, hello." She forced a smile and got to her feet.

"I'm Leon Clark." He put out his hand. "Pleased to meet you."

She became hideously aware of how sweaty her palms were. Should she shake his hand and leave him with that impression of her? Or pretend like she hadn't noticed him offering the handshake?

The seconds grew noticeably longer, and she realised she couldn't just leave him standing there with his hand held out. Quickly, she wiped her palm on the side of her skirt, and they shook while she prayed he hadn't noticed.

"Come this way."

He led her through the building, down a maze of corridors, until they reached what she assumed was his office. Someone else was already in there—a woman in her forties.

"This is my colleague, Kate Fowler," he introduced. "She'll be sitting in on the interview today."

Macie took a seat opposite and fished her CV out of her bag. "I brought this with me. I wasn't sure if you'd need it."

"Oh, no need. We've got everything online."

Her cheeks burned. "Right, of course."

He crossed his legs and steepled his fingers to his chin. "So, Miss Ostrow, tell me, why do you want to work for Direct Call?"

Macie reeled off some of the fictious reasons she'd been practising at home, which seemed to please both interviewers. They moved on to go through all the usual questions, asking her to give them examples of how she'd handled certain customer service situations. Most of what she replied with was completely made up, but she highly doubted these two were going to start doing investigative work to find out if some scenario from years ago was true or not. The interview felt as though it was going on forever, and then came the inevitable question.

"I can't help but notice you have a sizable gap in your CV," Mr Clark said.

She took a breath and nodded. "That's right. It wasn't by choice. I-I haven't been well."

His brow furrowed. "Oh? In what way, if you don't mind me asking?"

"I had a virus that left me with chronic heart disease, and I needed to have a heart transplant."

His eyes widened. "You had a heart transplant? That's pretty incredible."

"Yes, it is. I'm very lucky. I feel grateful every day just to be alive, and I make sure every day matters," she lied, "which is why I'll be an excellent employee if you were to hire me. I don't believe in doing anything half-hearted anymore."

He gave a laugh and pointed at her. "Half-hearted. Ha. Good one."

She hadn't intended it to be a pun, but she smiled along anyway.

"Well, I think we have everything we need, Miss Ostrow. We do have some other candidates to see, but we'll be in touch."

Macie nodded and stood. "Thank you for your time."

She didn't know if he was going to offer to shake her hand again and was grateful when he didn't. She turned and left the office. A moment later, laughter followed her out. Why were they laughing? Was it about her? Were they rolling their eyes at her and laughing at her bad answers?

Why hadn't he tried to shake her hand again? Oh God, had it been because it was really sweaty the first time? Had he wiped his palm against his trouser leg afterwards? How mortifying. And then there was that stupid comment about something being half-hearted. Would he realise that she'd never meant it as a joke, and be the one to kick himself about it? Why did she always end up overthinking and overanalysing every little moment? She'd thought the rest of the interview had gone well, but now she thought back, she couldn't remember what she'd said. Her mind was a complete blank. Had she babbled the whole way through with a load of nonsense?

She forced herself to keep going, heading down the corridor towards the exit, but her legs went weak beneath her, and she couldn't catch her breath. She passed huge offices with people sitting in booths, headsets on, the swell of talk and telephones ringing. Had she passed this way before, when she'd come in? She didn't think she had. And now she felt like they were all staring at her. They knew something was wrong with her. Dizziness swept over her, and the nausea returned. What if she threw up in front of everyone? She'd be mortified. But then a more serious worry took over. Her heart was beating too fast and too hard, and for a split second, it didn't beat at all.

Oh God. Was that an arrhythmia? Was the heart failing on her?

She stumbled and almost fell, just catching herself on the wall to prevent her hitting the floor. Pain stabbed at her chest. She couldn't breathe. A band wrapped around her rib cage and squeezed tighter, not allowing her lungs to expand or her heart to beat. She needed to call an ambulance. It was finally happening—the thing she'd been so sure would happen ever since the transplant. The heart was failing.

"Please, help," she managed to squeak right before she went down to her knees.

Footsteps pounded towards her, and suddenly she was surrounded by legs, and a bombardment of questions drowned out the ringing of phones.

"What's your name?"

"Are you okay?"

"What's happened?"

"Ambulance," she managed to rasp. "Call...ambulance."

# Chapter Ten

Ryan drove to the hospital, Mallory in the passenger seat beside him. The tip about the victim being sick with liver disease was too good a lead not to follow up. He'd been tempted to just get Mallory to go with one of the DCs to ask some questions, but the truth was that the hospital had a draw for him.

Cole Fielding had been moved out of the Intensive Care Unit but was still in the hospital. With no family who would want to care for a man in a minimally conscious state, he needed to stay where he was. Ryan had been doing his best to stay informed about Cole's recovery, but since his initial wakeup from the coma, it seemed Cole hadn't made much improvement. Ryan knew he shouldn't take pleasure from that, but he did. Maybe pleasure was the wrong word, but he wasn't sure how either he or Donna would be able to handle day-to-day life knowing that Cole was out there just living his, as though he hadn't taken the life of their innocent little girl. The thought of possibly bumping into Cole in town or in a restaurant would have made him feel as though he wouldn't have been able to breathe.

He glanced over at his sergeant as he drove. "How's it going with the care bloke then?"

She didn't look at him. "There's nothing going on."

He arched an eyebrow. "I thought he took you out to dinner the other night."

"He did, but it was just dinner, that's all." She grinned. "A lady doesn't kiss and tell."

"You trying to tell me you're a lady?"

She mock punched his arm.

"Hey!" Ryan protested. "I'm driving. And anyway, you deserve a decent bloke."

"You mean decent blokes exist?" She laughed at his expression. "I'm only joking. I'm sure there are some out there. It's just that my job doesn't make things easy, and neither does my home life. It'll take a pretty special bloke to want to take me on *and* my brother."

"Ollie is great! Any man would be lucky to have the both of you in his life."

"Try telling that to someone who just wants to have a bit of fun. "

"But this new guy knows your home life, and he knows your brother as well—really well by now, I'd imagine—so he knows exactly what he's getting into."

Mallory smiled. "That's all true, but I'm not going to get my hopes up. I've had men tell me in the past that they love Ollie and understand, but then the realities of having Ollie, together with the pressures of my job, makes them realise it's harder than they'd anticipated. They always end up wanting to be the centre of attention, and I simply can't give them that, so they scarper."

"This one might be different."

She shrugged. "I just want to be prepared when he's not."

"You sure you're not creating a self-fulfilling prophecy."

Mallory chuckled. "That sounds a little New Age for you."

"I just mean that you're preparing for him to let you down before you've even given him the chance to prove himself. You'll be looking out for reasons to give him the old heave-ho, so the minute the poor bloke puts a foot wrong, you'll be done with him."

"I'm not quite that callous," she protested.

"You have walls up, Mallory, and I totally understand why, but they're not going to help."

She snorted. "Like you're one to talk."

"I've already tried the marriage and family thing, and it didn't work out for me, as you know. I wouldn't put myself through it again."

"I'm sorry, boss."

He shot her a glance. "But you're younger and should have the chance to have these things in your life."

"Well, we'll see."

He pulled into the hospital car park and found a spot. They approached the main entrance. A large board listed all the different departments and which floors they were on.

"This way." He nodded in the direction of the hepatology unit.

Mallory walked alongside him. "We'll be lucky if we get a lead on this. We don't know if the man was local or how long it's been since he had his treatment—though the pathologist didn't think the scar was particularly old."

"It's the best lead we have, though, at least until we get a hit from misper."

They reached the hepatology department. It was busy, men and women in scrubs bustling about, patients in wheelchairs waiting for treatment. A man was talking to one of the nurses at the reception desk.

Ryan waited until he was finished and then stepped forward.

"Excuse me," Ryan said, getting the woman's attention. He showed her his ID. "I'm DI Chase. I wondered if you could help me? We're trying to track down the identification of a man who we believe was receiving treatment for his liver." He held the photograph up for the woman to see.

It wasn't easy showing a photograph of a dead man.

"We wondered if you recognised this man at all?"

Ryan hadn't had a huge amount of hope. How many people came through this ward every day? He had no idea. There were also a lot of staff, and this particular nurse might not have had any contact with their victim, even if he had been here.

But she surprised him.

"Yes, I do. He's spent a lot of time here over the past year or so. His name is Logan Foss."

"You know that for sure?"

"Absolutely. He's been in and out of here for a long time. You get to know patients like that. He's a good bloke." Her forehead furrowed. "Is he all right?"

That wasn't a question he was going to answer. Now they had a name, the first people who needed to be informed was his family.

"Do you know if Logan has any family? Is he married? Children?"

"No, nothing like that. His parents have been pretty involved with his treatment, though. They were with him a lot of the time."

"I don't suppose you might have contact details for his parents?"

The nurse clearly recognised his questions weren't leading to something good. If Logan had been all right, he could have given them his parents' contact details himself.

"Is he in the hospital somewhere? Is it to do with the transplant?"

Ryan tensed. "I'm sorry, what?"

"The transplant? Has the donor liver rejected?"

Ryan shot Mallory a look. This was a development. The liver that had been stolen hadn't originally belonged to the victim.

"No, it's nothing to do with that. How long ago did he have the transplant?"

She pursed her lips as she thought. "Oh, it's been a few months now. I thought he was doing well."

"Do you have the contact details for his parents?"

"Give me a minute."

She went to the computer and pulled her seat on wheels under her to sit down. Her fingers flew across the keyboard for a minute, and then she paused to jot something down on a piece of paper.

"Here you go." She stood back up to reach across the reception desk to hand it to Ryan.

"Thanks."

"Can you tell him Lexie from the hepatology unit said hi."

Ryan nodded, though that wasn't a promise he'd be able to keep. "Thanks for this." He waved the piece of paper. "You've been very helpful."

He may need to return to speak to her again once Logan Foss's parents had been informed of his death. He got the impression Lexie had created a bit of a bond with Logan during his time on the ward. Maybe she'd have some idea about who would have wanted Logan dead.

"Is it just me," Mallory said as they walked away, "or is this case getting stranger and stranger."

"It's not just you. I don't know what to think."

"He was a transplant patient," she mused out loud. "The liver the killer stole wasn't a damaged one. It was the one he'd received. Did whoever kill him and take the liver know that?"

Ryan shook his head. "I honestly have no idea. It seems like too much to be a coincidence, though."

"Could someone have been jealous? Another transplant patient maybe? What if they thought the liver should have gone to them and decided to take it anyway?"

Ryan arched his brow. "You're talking about someone who is life-threateningly sick abducting a man, killing him, and then dragging him out to the warehouse and performing a surgery on him that wouldn't even work. It wasn't as though they'd be able to use the liver themselves."

Mallory thought for a moment. "Okay, maybe it was a family member of someone who was waiting for a liver and didn't get it."

"It's a possibility," he had to admit. "Though it would also mean someone had access to that information. Let's get a list of people who were also in line to receive a transplant. Would the patients know who else was on the list?"

"They might do if they knew each other, perhaps they met in treatment and they talked."

Ryan nodded. "We need to talk to the doctors as well, find out exactly how this works. Does someone make a decision on who gets what, or is it just a first come, first served situation?"

"I'm pretty sure there's some kind of board who puts the patients up as candidates and then they all take a vote as to who is likely to give the liver its best chance of survival."

He thought on that for a moment. "Did someone out there get voted against and give them enough of a motive to kill Logan?"

They made their way back out of the hospital. Ryan experienced that same draw to the unit Cole Fielding remained on. He tried to remind himself that even though Cole was awake, he was in no way the same man who'd killed Hayley. Clearly, his brain function had been affected from the fall and the amount of time he'd spent unconscious, and there was no way of knowing if he'd ever regain any memory of what had happened leading up to the attempted hanging from the bridge, or, if he did remember, if he'd ever be able to communicate those events to another person.

"You okay, boss?" Mallory asked him.

He dragged himself from his thought. "Yes, fine. Just been a full-on day already."

"We're making progress, though," she assured him.

He didn't want to tell her that he hadn't even been thinking about the case. "Yes, we have. Now we know his identity, I'm sure things will snowball from here. Can you get word around to the rest of the team that we've got an ID on our victim? We need to run a background check on him, find out if he's got any history or was known to the police. At least now we can start looking at his background and trying to trace his final movements. I want to know everything there is to know about Logan Foss. What was Logan's job? Who were his family and friends? When was the last time someone saw him or heard from him? Did he have a mobile phone, and if so, what had happened to it?"

Mallory was already taking out her phone. "On it, boss."

They needed to check out Logan's home address, see if there was any sign of a struggle. Had Logan been abducted from somewhere and taken to the warehouse or had he agreed to meet someone there and gone of his own speed? The missing trainer made Ryan think someone had taken him there and he was most likely either unconscious or dead when that happened, since the sole of the sock had been clean. Had the trainer fallen off while he'd been dragged or carried. Had it come off inside a car?

The list of leads that needed to be followed grew bigger the more he thought about it.

First, they had the unenviable job of breaking this news to the victim's parents.

# Chapter Eleven

M r and Mrs Foss lived in a red-brick house on the outskirts of Clifton. It was an enviable area, with plenty of open green space and period properties that were worth a fair few quid.

Ryan pulled the unmarked car up outside of the house and looked up at it. The poor people inside were about to have their worlds shattered, and he always hated being the person to do it.

As of yet, no one had reported Logan Foss missing. It hadn't even been twenty-four hours since his body had been discovered, however, and he was a grown man, despite whatever medical issues he may have had, so his parents probably just thought he was getting on with his life.

"Ready?" he asked Mallory.

"As I'll ever be."

They both climbed out, and Ryan brushed the final crumbs off his suit from the sandwich they'd grabbed on the way over and eaten in the car. Together, they approached the painted red front door, and Ryan rang the bell.

A man answered, frowning at the two smartly dressed people on his doorstep, probably thinking they were going to try selling him something or asking him if he'd found God yet. "Yes?"

Ryan held up his ID. "Mr Foss?"

"I am."

"I'm DI Chase, and this is my colleague, DS Lawson. Can we come in for a moment?"

His frown deepened. "What's this about?"

"I'd really prefer not to talk about it on the doorstep. Is anyone else home?"

"Yes, my wife, Carol."

"Good. It would be best if we spoke to both of you together."

Alarm flashed across his face. "What's this about? Has something happened?"

Ryan gestured into the house. "Please, Mr Foss."

The older man turned and yelled into the bowels of the property, "Carol, police are here. You need to come down."

A woman in her sixties appeared at the top of the stairs. "Police? What do they want?"

"If everyone would come and sit down," Mallory said gently, "we can explain."

Carol Foss trotted down the stairs and joined them in the living room. Both of Logan's parents wore identical expressions of concern, and they sat side by side on the sofa.

"Mr and Mrs Foss," Ryan began, "the body of a young man was found in a warehouse just outside of Whitchurch late last night. I'm very sorry to tell you that we believe it to be your son, Logan."

Disbelief crossed Carol's face. "What? No, that can't be right."

"We will need you to do a formal identification, but I'm afraid it does appear to be Logan."

She shook her head repeatedly. "No, no, no. I don't believe you. You've got this wrong. Logan is fine." She twisted towards her husband. "Barry, phone him. Phone him right now. He'll answer, and you can speak to him yourself."

Barry's face was pale. "Carol, listen to what the police are saying to us."

"No, I won't. I refuse to because they're wrong! Someone like Logan doesn't go through everything in his life that he has only to end up dead in some warehouse. That's ridiculous. I won't believe it, I won't."

"I'm very sorry, Mrs—" Mallory started to say.

Carol lifted a hand to stop her. "Fine, if you won't phone him, I'll do it myself and then you'll see."

She got up and scurried off to find her phone. It was on the dining room table, and she swiped the screen, her hands trembling. She put the phone to her ear but only waited a moment before lowering it back down again.

"It just goes through to his answerphone." Her voice wavered.

"Come and sit back down, Carol," her husband said, tears in his blue eyes. He looked to Ryan. "You're sure it's him? There's no mistake?"

Ryan shook his head. "Of course, we'll want you to do a formal identification of his body, but I've seen him and his photograph. There's not a mistake."

Carole hadn't moved, so her husband got up and took her by the arm and led her back to the sofa.

Her hand to her mouth, she said, "Oh God, please don't let it be true. Let there be some other explanation."

No one could give her one, and she broke down, her face in her hands, her sob morphing into a howl. Her husband put his arm around her, clearly also distressed but working a lot harder to keep it in. It was a pattern Ryan saw often, how men—especially of the older generation—held in their emotions while in company, even when it came to something as soul-destroying as this. He knew because he'd been there himself.

Mallory got to her feet. "I'll make us all some tea."

They needed to question Logan's parents and they weren't going to be able to do so while his mother was so distressed. While her grief would be with her for the rest of her life, the shock would ease.

Mallory disappeared into the kitchen.

"How did he die?" Barry asked. "Was it because of the transplant? Did something go wrong?"

Ryan wasn't completely sure how to answer that. Could it be connected to the transplant? It certainly looked that way, though not in the way Logan's father was thinking.

"We're currently treating the death of your son as a murder investigation."

"Murder?" Barry said. "No, that can't be right. Who would want to murder our Logan?"

"That's what we're hoping to find out. Your knowledge about your son could help us figure out who did this to him."

Ryan thought, after suicide, murder must be the worst possible way to lose someone you loved. Even when someone died naturally, it was hard not to torture yourself about what they'd gone through as they'd taken their last breaths. And for someone to be murdered meant that they went through it without anyone they loved by their side or holding their hand. Losing Hayley had been the hardest thing he'd ever been through, but at least he'd been there. He'd seen exactly what had happened, and she'd died in his arms. At least he hadn't needed to torture himself with thoughts of what her final moments had been.

Barry stared at him. "You mean you don't know who killed him? They're still out there somewhere?"

"We're doing everything we can to find them," Ryan assured him.

Logan's father raised a finger. "Wait a minute. How was he murdered? How did someone kill him?"

Ryan didn't want to get into too much detail, especially with how distressed Mrs Foss was. At some point, they'd find out exactly what had happened, but it didn't need to be yet. He was thankful they hadn't been the ones to find their son's body in such a way. A person didn't stop being a child to a parent, even when they were fully grown. Ryan imagined these particular parents had been through more than most, living with a son who had been sick for so many years.

"He appears to have died from heart failure due to blood loss caused by a knife wound."

"He was stabbed?" Carol clutched her hand to her mouth. "Someone stabbed him?"

"Yes. I'm very sorry. We still have the pathologist working on the final post-mortem report."

Mallory returned with two cups of tea for the parents and set them on the coffee table. They would probably go undrunk, but it was a simple form of comfort—making someone a cup of tea when they'd received bad news.

Barry's chin trembled as he spoke. "We've always lived with the fear that we might lose him, but we'd never imagined it would be like this. Who would do something like that?"

"That's what we're trying to find out. If you could answer some questions for us about Logan, it would help a great deal."

"We'll do whatever you need us to, isn't that right, Carol?"

His wife didn't look as though she was in much of a state to help anyone, but Ryan hoped that would change as she came to terms with what had happened.

"When was the last time you saw Logan?" Ryan asked.

Barry laced his fingers together and gripped them hard, his knuckles turning white. "A couple of days ago. He came to the house and stayed for a cup of tea."

"How did he seem?"

"Fine. Just like his normal self. Chatty and happy. He was always such a positive person, even after everything he's been through in his life. Others might have let it get to them, but he didn't. He wasn't someone to ask 'why me' when he was sick. He used to say, 'why *not* me.' I guess he'd probably say the same thing now." He swiped a tear from his eye.

"Was he involved in anything like drugs or debt?"

Barry sat back in shock at the suggestion. "God no, Logan wasn't like that at all. He never would get involved with drugs—he'd know how harmful that would be. He didn't even drink alcohol. He was into his fitness, when he was strong enough to be. It was the most frustrating thing for him, after his diagnosis, that he couldn't run anymore, and he even struggled at the gym."

"Can you think of anyone who might have wanted to hurt your son?"

"No, not at all. He was a good man. Getting his new liver meant everything to him. He'd finally got a second chance at life, and he wanted to make the most of it."

Ryan changed the subject slightly. "You said he'd been sick for some time? Can you elaborate on that?"

"He had a genetic disorder that didn't get picked up until he was in his late teens. By the time the doctors realised what was going on, it had already caused a lot of damage. Logan managed things as best he could, but eventually it was decided the only way he stood any chance of survival was with a transplant."

"How long ago did he have the surgery?"

"It was three months ago now."

"And he was recovering from it well? No issues?"

Barry shook his head. "No, he was doing great."

"What about people he was close to? Did he have a girlfriend? Any significant other?"

"Not that we were aware of. We wanted that for him," Barry added, "but with him being so poorly for so long, I think he found it hard to make that kind of connection with someone."

"Friends?" Ryan checked.

"Yes, he had friends, but not a big group." Barry's eyes were leaking again, and he swiped at them with the ball of his hand. His nose and cheeks were red, a crackled red spiderweb of veins. "They were mainly a couple of lads who he knew from school who stuck around. Again, it's not easy being sick in your twenties. When everyone else is going to clubs and parties, or going off travelling, he was stuck at home."

Ryan took his notebook and pen out of his pocket and offered it to Barry. "Can I trouble you for the names and numbers of those he was close to? It's possible Logan opened up to them about something that might be important."

Barry nodded and took them. He quickly jotted down some names and handed it back to Ryan. Ryan glanced at it. There were only two names on there. He experienced a pang of sympathy for a man he'd never even known. Logan Foss had had a hard life and an even harder death.

Ryan tucked the notebook into his jacket pocket then folded his hands on the table. "Did Logan live alone? Or did he have any flatmates or anything?"

"No, he lived alone, though we helped him with the rent. His place isn't big, by any stretch of the imagination, but he wanted that independence at his age."

"That's understandable. We have police going to his flat now to search it. Hopefully, it'll give us some answers. What about a job? Did he work at all?"

Barry tilted his head from side to side. "On and off. It's not easy when you have a long-term illness to hold anything down. He was working at a sport's shop in town."

"Had he worked there for long?"

"Not long, just a few weeks and only part-time."

Ryan considered everything Logan's father had told them. He thought they had enough to go off for the moment, though they might need to return if more questions cropped up.

"Okay, thank you, Mr Foss. That's been very helpful. We will need one or both of you to come down to formally identify Logan's body, but you can do that when you're ready." Ryan glanced over at Carol Foss, who still had her hand covering her face, her shoulders shaking. "Again, I am very sorry for your loss. Please be assured that we will do everything in our power to find out who did this to your son."

Ryan got to his feet, and Mallory joined him. Barry also moved to stand, but Ryan put out his hand.

"Stay with your wife, we can see ourselves out."

# Chapter Twelve

Macie didn't need anyone to explain to her where she was. She'd woken up in hospital more times than she could count. Everything was familiar to her, from the beeping of the machines, to the underlying tang of cleaning product, to the rough texture of the sheets. They came to her gradually as she regained consciousness, and there was a strange sensation of coming home. Maybe this was where she was supposed to be after all.

Suddenly, she remembered what had happened, and a shot of adrenaline went through her.

Her heart!

It must still be beating, or she wouldn't still be alive. The paramedics must have restarted it, or maybe she'd had another operation? She shifted her body slightly but didn't experience the pain or tightness that came from waking up from an operation, and her head didn't hurt, nor was she nauseated. She knew how it felt to wake from a big op, and this wasn't it.

*I'm okay. I'm okay.*

She blinked open her eyes to the unnaturally bright glare of the strip lights overhead. Just like the smell of the place and feel of the sheets, the view of the ceiling was also familiar. How many days and nights had she lain in a bed exactly like this one, staring at an identical ceiling?

"She's awake, John."

Her mother's voice came from the other side of the room, and Macie turned her face towards it.

"Mum?"

Instantly, her mother was by her side. A moment later, her father appeared beside her.

Her dad took her hand. "You gave us a fright."

"What—what happened?"

"We're not sure, darling. The doctors have run some tests. They're going to be back in a minute to let us know."

"I remember being at the interview, and then my heart stopped beating. I passed out." Macie felt herself growing more panicky by the second.

Her mother squeezed her hand. "You're okay now, though. That's what matters."

The flash of a white coat at the door signalled a doctor entering the room. It was Dr Sharmen, one of the doctors who'd taken care of her over the course of her treatment and transplant, and Macie let out a sigh of relief upon seeing him. She trusted him to tell her the truth and not try to sugarcoat the outcome of whatever had happened to her back at the interview. If she was going to die, he would tell her. To her surprise, she discovered it would be a relief in some ways. At least then all the expectation would be gone. She'd be back to being a dying woman, and no one would think she should go on to live a fulfilling life. If she spent day after day in bed, no one would tell her she'd feel better if only she got up and had a shower and took some exercise. People would understand. Her outside would match how she felt inside.

She pushed herself up higher on the bed. The hospital gown gaped slightly, and she caught sight of the hideous scar she hated so much. She was still amazed they hadn't opened her up again, but perhaps that was what Dr Sharman was here to tell her—that she'd need to go back into surgery.

"Hello, Macie. How are you feeling?"

"Scared," she admitted.

He nodded. "That makes sense, but you really don't have anything to be frightened of. We've run an ECG, and your heart is beating perfectly normally. There's nothing to worry about."

She shook her head. "No, it wasn't beating normally. I felt it. I had a stabbing pain in my chest, and I couldn't breathe."

He perched on the edge of her bed like a friendly uncle coming to visit. They knew each other well. She'd been in and out of hospital for years now.

"Macie, what you experienced was a panic attack. Your mother said you were there for a job interview? I believe it all just got a bit too much for you, and your body let you know that by way of a panic attack."

"No, I've had panic attacks before. That was nothing like this. I thought I was going to die."

"Panic attacks can be felt in a number of different ways, at all kinds of intensities."

"But—but I passed out. I've only just woken up now."

"That happens, too, especially for someone who's been through as much physical and mental trauma as you have. The brain and body just can't cope with the amount of stress it's under and they simply shut down. It's like an extreme way of finally getting a rest."

She closed her eyes briefly. "This is crazy. I must be insane."

"You're perfectly normal, Macie, or at least as normal as anyone can be, considering what you've been through."

"She's very hard on herself, Doctor Sharmen," her mother said. "We keep telling her there's no rush to get back into things. She can take as much time as she needs."

"Your mother is right. Take it easy. You don't need to be doing things like job interviews at this early stage."

"I want to earn my own money. I'm twenty-seven and I still live at home with my parents."

"And you'll always be welcome, Macie," her father said.

Macie sighed. "I know, and I love you both, and I'm so grateful to have you. I guess I won't be getting that job anyway, considering I passed out in their corridor and they had to call an ambulance for me." She covered her face with her hands, and the drip threaded into the back of one of them tweaked. "God, how embarrassing."

It had only been a job answering phones. How hard would that have been? She'd been sure she could have managed it, and maybe even been good at it...perhaps. But it didn't matter what she thought. What mattered was how she'd conducted herself at the interview, and if the interviewers had housed any doubts about her health hampering her ability to do the job, she'd certainly proven to them that they were right.

"Don't be embarrassed, darling," her mum said. "It wasn't your fault. You certainly gave us all a fright, though."

Macie ducked her head, staring down at her hands on the white bedsheets. "Sorry."

Her mother took her fingers in hers. "You don't need to be sorry. Not for anything. None of this is your fault. We're so incredibly proud of you for how you've handled everything you've been through, and we're just glad you're okay."

Tears blurred Macie's vision. "I haven't handled it well, though, have I? What's even been the point of it all? I can't even get a job without passing out after the interview."

"It was just too much for you at the moment. That's all. You've been through more than any woman at your age should, and you need to cut yourself some slack. You're far too hard on yourself."

"I feel like I'm wasting it," she admitted.

Her mother frowned. "Wasting what?"

"The heart. This amazing gift was given to me, and what am I doing with it? Nothing. Just sitting in the house all day and going online and watching Netflix. I feel like the donor or their family would be so disappointed if they knew it was me who'd received it."

"No, they wouldn't. Don't be so silly."

"You don't know that."

Her mother's expression grew fierce. "Yes, I do. You're a beautiful, intelligent, caring young woman who now has her whole life ahead of her. Anyone would be proud to know their loved one's heart went to you."

"You're biased, Mum. What about these people who are going through transplant surgery and are still out there running marathons or climbing mountains and raising a ton of money for charity?"

They were everywhere, these people, on the news, across social media, in all her transplant forums. She only felt worse every time a new one popped up. What kind of despicable person was she to resent others for doing well—for raising money for charity, charities that were aimed at helping people like her—and all she felt was resentful towards them. They only helped to highlight how utterly useless she was.

"I don't care. We still have you in our lives, and no matter what you think, that's the most wonderful thing in the world to us. So even if you can't bring yourself to be happy about things right now, maybe you can be happy for us instead."

"I'll try. I just hate feeling like I'm letting everyone down."

Her mother's tone softened. "Who are you letting down, sweetheart?"

She flapped a hand helplessly. "Everyone. My donor. Their family."

"Maybe you should think about writing a letter to the transplant centre. They can pass it on to the donor's family, if they want to make contact."

"Oh, I couldn't do that. What would I even say?"

"Thank you," she suggested, "and everything you've said to me now. I bet you'd discover that they're far more accepting of your struggles than you give them credit for."

It would be a handwritten letter, that was all. A few simple words on a piece of paper. But even then, she didn't know what to say. She couldn't possibly tell them the truth about how she was feeling. They'd want to believe in some kind of fairy-tale where their loved one's heart had gone to one of those people climbing mountains and raising money for charity, or perhaps to a single parent with small children who now wouldn't have to grow up alone.

A tear slipped down her cheek, and she wiped it away with the back of her hand. "I'll think about it."

"Good."

The doctor stepped in. "You're free to go home as soon as you're ready, Macie. You don't need any more tests, and I don't think we need to monitor you further."

She blinked. "Are you sure?"

"Yes, I'm sure. You're fine. Like I said, it was a panic attack. Your heart is strong, and I don't have any concerns."

Macie sniffed. "I think the heart is probably stronger than I am."

"You *are* strong. Like your mother says, you need to stop being so hard on yourself."

But it didn't seem to matter what anyone else said to her. She couldn't shift the feeling that she was losing a game she couldn't stop playing.

# Chapter Thirteen

After a busy day researching, Tova left work but didn't go straight home. Instead, she stopped at the Park View Care Home.

Her grandmother, Marjory, was ninety-six years old and had outlived her own daughter, something that had been a great source of heartache. It had brought Tova and Marjory even closer, however, and it had killed Tova to put her grandmother in this home a little over eight years ago. But she hadn't been able to live independently any longer, and Tova didn't have the time to be able to watch her grandmother every minute of the day. After a couple of falls, where she'd been unable to get up for hours on end, and one scary incident involving the gas being left on and the neighbours complaining, Tova had been left feeling as though she didn't really have much of a choice. She'd heard so many scare stories about bad care homes, and the patients being neglected and the staff not caring, that she'd felt like she was betraying her grandmother or abusing her in some way. But their experience with this home had been the complete opposite. Everyone had been wonderful, and Marjory had settled in almost right away.

"Hi, Nonna." Tova leaned in to place a kiss to her grandmother's soft papery cheek. "You look pretty today."

"Jasmine came in to do everyone's hair," one of the staff said from beside them. She raised her voice slightly. "Isn't that right, Marjory? Jasmine came and did your hair?"

Tova's grandmother patted the white curls on her head. "Yes, she did. I think she did a good job, don't you?"

"It looks lovely." Tova smiled. "She did an excellent job." She pushed a cardboard box into her grandmother's hands. "Here, I brought you some of those cinnamon buns you like."

Her face brightened. "Oh, how wonderful. You do know how to spoil me, Tova."

They were only buns from a local bakery, but her grandmother seemed to think they were the height of sophistication and loved them. Tova made special trips just to get them for her.

"Don't go eating them all at once."

"I won't." Marjory turned to the nurse nearby. A badge attached to the other woman's shirt announced her name as April. "You've met my granddaughter, Tova, haven't you? She's on the telly, you know?"

The nurse, April, smiled. "I thought I recognised you from somewhere. You seem different in real life."

"I don't have a makeup artist living at my house." She gestured to her face. "This is far more natural than I'm allowed on the television. Honestly, they just plaster it on."

"Well, you're beautiful, no matter what. I saw that episode you did the other week of transplant recipients finding their donor's families." April clutched her hand to her chest. "My God, that was an emotional episode."

"Oh, it really was. We got great feedback from that show. We're going to be doing another one—it's already in the research phase. I've been working on it all day."

April settled in the seat beside Tova. "How do you research something like that? I thought that kind of thing was anonymous."

"Yes, it is, but in a city as small as Bristol, it's actually not so hard. Organs need to be used for transplant within a very short timeframe to make the transplant viable, so if something has happened like a road traffic accident where the victim hasn't opted out of organ donation, it can be easy to link that victim to the patients who all get the call the same day or night that a match has been found for them. In this particular case, it was the donor's family who wanted to find all the different people who their loved one's organs had gone to, and so they came on my programme."

April frowned. "I thought they could write to the recipients, if they wanted."

"They can write to the transplant centre, but unless the recipient also wants to make contact, they won't necessarily meet."

"But they did in this case?"

"Yes, with a little help, and we were able to arrange for that to happen. It meant a lot to the donor's family, to be able to tell the recipient about the person who'd saved their life, and for them to feel as though a part of them still lived on."

"It was wonderful," April gushed. "I'm not ashamed to admit that I shed a tear or two."

"So did I. Now we're hoping to unite them with more of the recipients. We just have to find them. Of course, not all of them will want to be found, and we'll respect that, but from experience, it seems to be very healing for all involved to meet."

April seemed to consider this for a moment. "It must be hard as well, though. A person had to die in order for them to live. It must be difficult for the recipient to come face to face with the fact people are grieving because of something they benefited from."

Tova nodded. "Yes, that's why some people prefer to stay anonymous. It's completely understandable, if that's the case, and we never push someone to get involved if they don't want to be."

"Well, I do hope you find others and do some more reunions. Like I said, I am such a big fan." She turned to Tova's grandmother. "You must be so proud of your granddaughter."

"Oh, I am." Marjory lifted one of the cinnamon buns as though in a toast. "She's a wonderful baker."

Tova smiled and patted the back of Marjory's hand. Her skin was so soft and warm. Tova's heart swelled with love. She knew her grandmother wouldn't have many more years to go, and every moment felt precious. Her nonna was her only living relative, and the thought of losing her, too, left her with a sense of being untethered to the world. She'd always thought by her age of forty-two, she'd have started a family of her own by now, but it had never happened that way. She'd had a couple of longer relationships, but they'd always ended badly. One had cheated on her for most of their relationship, and it had all but killed her self-esteem. The trust issues she'd carried from it had wrecked the next relationship because she'd been so paranoid about what her boyfriend was doing when she wasn't around that she'd driven him away. After that, she'd convinced herself she didn't need anyone else, and that she was an independent woman with an increasingly successful career and that was how it should be. But then she'd blinked and suddenly she wasn't in her early thirties anymore, she was approaching her late thirties and then tipping into her forties, and she'd started to feel as though her desperation seeped from her pores. Casual dating no longer existed. She was sizing up every man to see if he was potential marriage material, and men didn't like that—at least, the ones she'd met didn't.

Tova sat with her grandmother for a while longer, until it was time for dinner to be served up, and then she kissed her goodbye. She left the care home and drove the fifteen minutes to her flat. It was already dark, and she found herself looking forward to the end of the month when the clocks went forward and the evenings would be lighter.

She parked the rental vehicle outside her flat. Her Audi wasn't ready yet, and she discovered she was thankful for it. Did she even want the car back again? She'd loved driving it, but now she felt like it stood out too much. She might as well have a glowing neon sign above her head announcing to everyone who she was and where she lived. Perhaps she should trade it in for something less flashy.

As she approached her front door, she drew to a halt.

Something had been left on her doorstep.

A card with her name written across the front.

She frowned and stooped down to pick it up. She glanced over her shoulder, certain someone had been watching her, but the road was empty. Across the street were more flats, and she scoured the windows, trying to spot anyone standing in one of them, watching her. Nothing caught her attention, however.

She'd have thought she was just imagining things, but after the graffiti on her car and now this card, she didn't think she was overreacting.

Quickly, she tore open the envelope and pulled out the card. It was a 'thank you' card. From one of the guests she'd had on her show, perhaps? That was most likely, but she didn't like the idea of one of them knowing where she lived. It was hard to keep anything a secret these days. Even though she was careful online to never post anything that might give her address away, such as photographs taken outside her building, or pictures of letters or boxes that might have her address written on them, people could find out anything if they dug hard enough.

She opened up the card. The printed text was in a swirly font, written by the card designer, and said, '*Thanks for all your help,*' and, handwritten below that were the words, '*Who's next?*'

Immediately, she knew this was from the same person who was responsible for the graffiti. Who the hell were they? What did they want? They were implying she'd helped them with something, but she had no idea what that meant. And as for who was next...next for what?

She suddenly felt vulnerable and exposed, standing out here on her doorstep alone. Moving quickly, she fumbled with her keys, unlocking her front door. She stepped inside and slammed the door shut behind her, her heart racing. This wasn't like her at all. She didn't get spooked by things. She'd lived in this city her whole life, and she'd never felt defenceless like she did now.

She needed to report the card to the police.

Crossing into her kitchen, she placed her handbag on the table and scooped out her phone.

She was about to dial triple nine, but she paused. This was hardly an emergency, was it? She couldn't call to tell them about a thank-you card. Nothing about the card said 'threatening', yet that was how she took it. She'd already reported the damage to her car, but would they even think it was connected? They'd probably charge her for wasting police time, after all, the police were really busy and chronically underfunded. She was sure they had more important things to deal with.

Tova remembered something she'd seen in the news. Hadn't there been a body found just outside of the city last night—a murder investigation? In her previous job working for the papers, she'd have been on the scene herself, hoping to get a scoop on the story. Now, as much as she loved her job, it did sometimes feel like she was working on stories that would be better fitting to a woman's magazine than a real, hard-hitting newspaper. But she touched people, and that mattered, too. At least that's what she kept trying to tell herself.

No, she wouldn't call the emergency number, but she could report it, nevertheless. They already had a record of the graffiti, so they could add this new development to the case file.

Still, she couldn't bring herself to call. She imagined the police rolling their eyes at her as she tried to explain that it was the same language used on the graffiti, and that no one should know where she lived.

"Damn it."

She threw the card down on the table and turned to the fridge to pour herself a glass of wine. She kept a bottle in there for emergency situations—which was normally a bad day at work—but she figured this qualified, too.

For once, she wished she had a man in her life. She'd feel better if she had someone else here and it wasn't just her.

With the glass of wine in hand, she made her way around the flat, ensuring each of her doors and windows were locked. They were, just as she'd known they'd be. At least she hadn't found the card already *inside* the flat. That would have really freaked her out. It meant whoever had left it for her didn't have access to the place, so she was safe in here.

She needed to catch up on the research for the next show. She knew a couple of journalists who'd ended up on-screen who had someone else do all their research for them, and they just read out what they were given, but she preferred to be involved from the ground up. It meant she was still doing her job and wasn't only employed because of a pretty smile and her blonde hair.

Carrying her laptop and glass of wine to the sofa, she sat, tucking her legs up under her. The flat seemed too quiet, so she put on the television for a bit of background noise.

She forced herself to focus on her work, but her mind kept drifting back to the card.

Someone had been to her flat. Someone had gone to her place of work and graffitied her car.

What would they do next?

# Chapter Fourteen

Mallory managed to escape the office after Ryan's final briefing for the day. The search on Logan Foss's flat hadn't revealed any sign of violence, but his phone had been found there and sent off to Digital Forensics to unlock. His keys had also been located at the flat, and the front door had been unlocked, suggesting he was either taken from the flat by force or else had left in a rush. SOCO were working on the place now, and nearby CCTV had been requested so they could try and work out Logan's final movements.

She had a reason for wanting to be home at a reasonable time. She'd played down her relationship with Oliver's part-time respite carer, Daniel Williamson, but the truth was that they'd been out a few times now, and tonight they had another date.

Mallory stood in front of the mirror in her skinny black jeans and considered putting some of her piercings back in. In the end, she decided she couldn't be bothered—she'd only have to take them back out again. Outside of work, when she managed to get out to socialise, people never believed that she was a detective. Maybe it was because she appeared younger than she was, or most likely it was the slightly edgy way she dressed. Depending on her mood, she either took it as a compliment or an insult.

"You look pretty," Ollie told her from the doorway. "Are you going on a date with Daniel?"

She smoothed down the front of her equally black top. "Yeah, I am. Is that okay with you?"

Ollie shrugged. "I don't mind, if you like him."

"Do *you* like him, Ollie?"

"I like him. He asks lots of questions, though."

Mallory turned to face her brother. "He does?"

"Yes, about you. I like talking about you, but sometimes he gets boring."

"Talking about me gets boring?" Mallory discovered herself suppressing a smile.

"I like to talk about you, Mallory. I like to say what you like to eat and what music you listen to, but he wants to talk about your job. I like to talk about that, too, sometimes. I like that you're a detective like on the TV, but I don't really know what you do."

Mallory sat on her bed and patted the side as an invite for Ollie to join her. She wasn't sure how she felt about Daniel querying Ollie for information about her job. In a way, she was pleased he was interested, but why ask Oliver about that kind of thing and not her? Of course, her work got brought up on the odd occasion, but not enough for her to think he was overly interested. So why was he quizzing Ollie?

"What kind of things does he ask you, Ollie?"

Ollie gave his customary shrug. "Dunno. Boring stuff."

She didn't want to worry Ollie about it. This was a conversation she needed to have with Daniel over dinner. The thought made her uncomfortable, as though she was going to have to interrogate her date, but Ollie was her number one priority, and she didn't want Daniel making him uncomfortable either.

It was in her nature to be suspicious of people. Was Daniel just trying to mine Ollie for information so he would have something to talk to her about when they were together? It wasn't as though she'd ever share anything in detail about her cases with her brother anyway. Yes, sometimes he asked. He saw things on the local news and internet and asked her if she was working on the person who'd gone missing or the person who'd been killed, and sometimes she said yes and sometimes she said no. Normally, that was enough for Ollie, but on the odd occasion he wanted to know more, and so she told him without divulging anything that might be of importance to the case.

"Would you like me to ask him to stop?"

"Yes, please."

Mallory smiled. "I will then. To be honest, I find most of my work really boring, too. Lots of time sitting behind a desk doing paperwork."

"I like doing my puzzles better."

"So would I, buddy. So would I."

The doorbell rang, and Mallory got to her feet. "Right. How do I look?"

"Really pretty."

She wasn't quite sure she'd ever describe herself as being pretty—she had a slightly harsh appearance with overly sharp features, and her dyed black hair too poker straight and her fringe cut too short—but she appreciated Ollie's compliment.

Leaning in, she gave him a hug. "I've got my phone with me, and I'll only be two hours, no more, I promise."

Mallory hoped nothing related to the case would come up in that time. Though they were allowed time off, she always felt guilty not working when they were in the middle of something big. Her boss had a habit of working until as late as possible and only going home to sleep, but it wasn't as though he had anyone at home waiting for him. Everyone kept telling her that she needed time out from either taking care of Ollie or working, because she wouldn't be any good to anyone if she burnt out.

Ollie had been better recently when it came to his nightmares. It seemed time was a great healer, as the frequency of the nightmares had gone from almost every night, to only once and week and sometimes not even that. Her brother had begun to regain the confidence that he'd lost during the fire, and that made Mallory happy, too.

Aware she'd left Daniel standing on the doorstep, she hurried down to answer the door. At first, she couldn't see his face—it was hidden by the large bunch of flowers in his hand.

"These are for you." He thrust the bunch towards her.

"Oh, wow. Thanks. You didn't need to do that." Her cheeks flushed with heat. Things like flowers made her uncomfortable. She never quite knew what to do with them. "I'd better put them in some water quickly. Come in for a sec."

He was in their house at least a couple of times a week when he came to sit with Daniel, so it wasn't unusual to have him in her home. The change in dynamic due to the reason he was there, though, made her awkward. She wasn't good at this kind of thing, she decided. She wasn't sure she even had a vase to put the bloody flowers in. She stood in her kitchen, hoping an option might materialise in front of her. Was he going to realise that she was a bit of a failure as far as femininity went? She'd much rather be standing in a morgue than a florist.

"Umm, I'll sort them out when I get back," she said eventually, dumping the stalks of the flowers into the kitchen sink, sticking the plug in, and running the cold tap for a moment.

"Sure. How's Ollie?"

"He's good. He's probably sitting at the top of the stairs, waiting to say bye."

She stuck her head around the corner, and sure enough, there he was.

"Two hours," she told him again. "And we're just at the pub around the corner if you need anything. You can call me, and I'll be back with a few minutes."

He nodded. "I know, Mallory." Then he must have remembered Daniel. "Hi, Daniel. You have to bring her back in two hours."

Daniel grinned and did a little salute. "Got it."

Mallory let them both out of the house, and they walked around the corner to where the Pig and Pumpkin was located.

The pub was busy, but they'd booked a table. It was the sort of place that sold local beer and made a plate of fish and chips look classy. Mallory finally started to relax. They were shown over to their table, but they'd have to order at the bar and give their table number.

"I'll grab some drinks," Daniel said. "Beer? Wine? Something stronger?"

"I think I'll leave the hard stuff until after I've eaten. Can I have half a lager for now?"

"No problem."

She resisted checking her phone, either for calls from Ollie or any developments on the case. Had the search teams located the missing trainer or even the murder weapon yet? If not, what had happened to them? Had the killer kept them for a souvenir, or had they not even noticed Logan Foss had lost his trainer and it was still stuffed in their car boot or something?

Daniel returned within a few minutes with their drinks, and she forced herself to stop thinking about work.

"Cheers," she said, at the same time Daniel said it, and they clinked glasses together.

Mallory took a sip of her beer. "Ollie mentioned that you've been asking him about my work a lot."

Daniel frowned. "Have I?"

She raised her eyebrows. "I don't know, I'm not there when it's happening. I'm just telling you what Oliver said."

He squared his shoulders, but he didn't meet her eye. "I don't think I have. I mean, if I've seen something on the news that I think you might have been involved in, I guess I've mentioned it to him."

"Just mentioned it? He seems to feel you're drilling him for information."

That wasn't quite how her brother had put things, but something about this was feeling off. Was she just being overly suspicious? Daniel gave her the impression he was feeling guilty about it. Maybe he was just embarrassed that he'd been pulled up on it. He might have been trying to get information from Ollie.

She didn't want to cause problems. He'd been a godsend to her over the past few months when Ollie had been having all those nightmares and she'd been desperate for a break. And

Oliver liked him. They got on well, and she didn't want to spoil that. If she asked Helping Hands for someone different, they might send over an older woman who Ollie wouldn't feel as comfortable with as he did another man of his own age.

It suddenly occurred to her that going out with Daniel like this was a very selfish thing to do. If she and Daniel fell out for any reason, then she'd be taking him away from Ollie.

"Forget I said anything," she backpedalled, though it wasn't in her nature to do so. "Just thought I'd mention it so that Ollie doesn't feel like he's being bored because of me."

Daniel relaxed a fraction. "Of course." His lips tweaked in a smile. "I'll be sure not to mention you too much in future. It's just hard not to when someone is on your mind."

His words only increased her discomfort, and she picked up her menu and buried her face in it to hide.

# Chapter Fifteen

Ryan had slept surprisingly deeply. He didn't know if the rest was the result of finding out about Donna getting the all-clear or if it was because he had only managed a couple of hours the previous night due to being out at the crime scene. Either way, the sleep had done him good, and he went back into the office with a renewed sense of determination that they were going to track down whoever was responsible for killing Logan Foss.

The first thing he did was call a briefing with his team.

"We had some significant developments with the case yesterday, namely in finding out the identity of the victim." Several new photographs and names had been added to the evidence board behind him, including the location of Logan Foss's flat, his place of work, and the route he'd most likely taken to get between one and the other. "Logan Foss was twenty-nine years old, single, and a recent recipient of a liver transplant which was needed because of a genetic condition he was born with which resulted in liver failure. He had the operation three months ago and had been doing well, according to his doctors, but on the first of March, Logan was abducted and murdered, and that liver was stolen.

"It's unlikely the liver was taken for the black market, but that's still a possibility. Despite it not being a viable liver, there's a chance whoever did this was an amateur or perhaps was disturbed during the killing. However, there might be another motive. Was someone upset that Logan got the liver when perhaps they or a loved one didn't? Though these things are confidential, I'm sure patients get talking, and perhaps someone found out and didn't like it."

Ryan paced across the front of the room.

"We've had SOCO at Logan's flat. He lived alone. It appears that he may have either left from there or was taken, as his front door was unlocked, and his keys and phone were found inside, though there was no obvious sign of violence, and so far, no blood has been found. Now, we know that he left work," Ryan pointed at the position of the sports shop on the map, "shortly after six. This area should be well covered by CCTV, and we know he went home, so let's trace his exact route. Was he alone? Was anyone following him?"

He looked around at the faces of his team. "Who was tasked with going over the CCTV from the near the warehouse from the night of his murder?"

DC Linda Quinn raised a hand. "I was, boss, but I'm afraid I haven't come across anything that would be of any use so far."

"That's okay. Can you refocus on the CCTV from between his place of work to his flat?"

"No problem."

Ryan continued. "His mobile phone is with Digital Forensics, and we've requested his phone records as well, so hopefully that'll give us some idea who he was in contact with in the days and hours leading up to his death." He focused on one of his other DCs. "Shonda, can I get you to find out what you can about Logan online as well. Take a look at his social media accounts, that kind of thing."

He addressed the two men on his team. "I want Logan's neighbours all interviewed. Find out if they saw or heard anything unusual from around the time Logan went missing. See if anyone saw him get home. Find out if he was alone or if he was joined by someone else later. I want his colleagues spoken to, as well. What kind of mood was Logan in when he left work? Did he mention any plans he may have had?"

Heads nodded.

Mallory put up her hand. "Boss, I thought you should know that we've had the forensics report come through from the crime scene. According to the report, the blood spatter indicated that the victim was still alive when the initial stab wound was made. There was a single region where no blood was located on the concrete warehouse floor which indicates the position where the attacker must have stood."

"So, there would have been blood on the killer's skin and clothes," Ryan surmised.

"That's right." Mallory continued, "No other blood type was located, so the assailant wasn't injured during the attack. No sign of any other bodily fluids located on scene either."

Ryan hadn't thought this was a sexually motivated killing, but it was always possible. At least the forensics had ruled that out.

She continued to go through the report. "Several different types of unidentified DNA was located in the warehouse, together with several different fingerprints lifted. One set located on the warehouse doors were later matched to Cameron James. The warehouse has been a working unit until recently, therefore the prints and DNA could easily have been present prior to the murder. We have a couple of partial footprints in the blood, one of which is so far unmatched to anyone who we know was on the scene, so there's a chance that belongs to our killer. It's been estimated as a male shoeprint, size ten, which can give a very approximate estimation of a height of around six feet, but as you know, it's not an exact science."

"Thanks for that." Ryan clapped his hands together. "Right, let's get on with things then. We have a lot of ground to cover."

The team dispersed, and Ryan went to his DCI's office to fill her in on where they were with the case. He'd worked with Mandy Hirst for several years now, and she was good at letting him just get on with things. Happy that he'd brought her up to speed on everything, he left the office to find an excited DC Dawson rushing towards him. Shonda's dark eyes shone, and she grinned at him, exposing her small white teeth and a little too much gum.

"I did a search of Logan Foss's name, and you won't believe what came up."

"A website written by his killer admitting everything?" Ryan said, only half-jokingly. That would certainly make his job easier.

"Not quite, but almost as big. Let me show you."

He followed her back to her desk and stood behind her as she hit 'play' on her computer, and a video started. To Ryan's surprise, there was Logan Foss sitting on a stool onstage. He wasn't alone. A short blonde woman in her late thirties to early forties held a microphone out to him.

"What is this?" Ryan asked.

"It's a television show that's on weekly called *Tova's Questions*. It does investigatory stories, like the other week it did an exposé on toxic masculinity. Another week it did something on women who were forced to give their babies up for adoptions back in the fifties and sixties. It's kind of people-focused investigative journalism, mixed with a bit of a women's magazine layout."

"And they had Logan on the show?"

She nodded. "Yep. Just a few weeks ago."

"Could this be connected to the case?"

"Well, you know how you were saying about the transplants being anonymous? Logan clearly waived that anonymity because he talks about his liver transplant. In fact, the whole reason he was on the show was to meet his donor's family."

Ryan frowned. "But how did they find him in the first place?"

"I'm not sure. I guess we'll need to speak to the production team about that."

He pointed at the screen, to the small blonde woman. "Remind me of her name again?"

"That's Tova Lane. I believe she started out as a newspaper journalist and then had some contacts in television and got her debut on-screen. She's a bit of a minor celebrity around here."

Celebrity culture definitely wasn't something Ryan had ever followed. "If she interviewed Logan, there's a possibility he might have told her something that could help us."

"We should arrange to speak to her," Shonda said. "I'll watch through the television show featuring Logan as well, find out exactly what happened."

"No, let me do that, or we'll do it together. What better way to get a feel for a victim than watching him on-screen?"

He'd never be able to meet Logan in person, so this was the next best thing.

"Let's watch it now, if you have time?"

He checked his watch. "I've got time. Should we get some popcorn in?"

She laughed and hit 'play' on the show.

It was strange seeing Logan Foss alive and well. And he did look well. At a glance, you would never know that he'd been going through some serious health struggles and been close to death. He seemed like any other twenty-something male—casually dressed in jeans and white trainers. They might even be the same ones he'd been wearing when he'd been killed. The trainer that was missing.

Onstage, Logan took a seat on a stool opposite the petite blonde woman who was the show's host. He seemed a little nervous, flustered by the blonde, despite the age difference. She smiled brightly, leaned over to touch his knee, and then introduced him to the audience, who applauded. She got Logan talking about his journey, how he'd first shown signs of liver disease as an adolescent. She commented how people automatically assumed it was an older person's disease, perhaps even that of an alcoholic, but he corrected her in that his illness was inherited. He'd lived with it for years without knowing, and it wasn't until he was a teenager that he'd developed a cough, which the doctors had initially put down to exercise-induced asthma, and then he'd gradually got worse, getting repeated lung infections. Eventually, he'd had a scan, and they'd discovered his liver was so badly damaged that he would need a transplant if he was going to survive.

"And that's where your donor comes in?" Tova Lane said.

He nodded. "That's right. I literally wouldn't be here today if it wasn't for my donor. Words will never explain how grateful I am, and how grateful my parents are. I got a whole new chance at life."

"Would you like to meet your donor's family?"

He blinked, his eyes bright. "Yes, I would."

She reached out and squeezed his hand. "That's wonderful, because they'd love to meet you, too. Let me introduce Clare McIver and her children, Martha and Simon."

Tova glanced backstage, and they both rose to their feet as a woman and two children, who were around the ages of twelve and fourteen, walked onto the stage. The woman, who was in her late forties, her dark hair curly and white at the temples, opened up her arms to Logan as though she was greeting a long-lost relative.

The audience got to their feet, clapping and cheering the emotional moment. The camera swept across them and then focused in on someone wiping tears from her eyes, just to push across the point that people were moved by what was happening onstage.

While the camera had been panning the audience, runners must have brought in more stools as, by the time they came back to the people onstage, the donor's wife had taken a seat next to Logan, and her children were on her other side.

"How hard must it be for the kids to go through that?" Shonda said, interrupting the show. "Why has the mother dragged them onto a television show not long after their father has died?"

"Maybe she thought it would be healing for them to see that their dad is still living on in some way."

"But their dad wasn't a liver. The bits of you aren't what makes you who you are. It's just an organ. A piece of meat."

Ryan could see where she was coming from, but he also understood the need for people to give terrible situations meaning. He and Donna hadn't been able to face having Hayley cut up and pieces of her dished out to others at the time, and it was something he regretted. They should have helped others out of their daughter's death. But at the time, it had all been so utterly raw and devastating, neither of them had been able to see or think about anyone or anything outside of their own grief, and after she'd been killed, he hadn't wanted anyone to touch another single hair on her head.

"People need to make sense of a terrible situation."

She shot him a sympathetic smile. "Yes, of course. Sorry."

Ryan turned his attention back to the show.

Tova Lane was interviewing the donor's wife now. "Tell us a little about your husband, Gregory. What kind of man was he?"

Clare's face lit up. "Greg was a wonderful man. He was a local vicar and was much loved in his parish. He adored his family, too. We miss him desperately, but we know he's with God now."

Behind them, a big photograph of a man in his late forties appeared. It was a close-up of his face, but not so close they couldn't make out the dog-collar. He had a wide, open smile, and creases at the corners of his eyes. He looked like someone who people would want to open up to.

"It's so wonderful to know that a piece of him continues to live on in Logan," Tova Lane said.

"That's how we like to think of it, too."

"Tell everyone a bit about how the two of you met."

"We were childhood sweethearts. We met at secondary school, and though we didn't become a couple until we were both seventeen, we were the only people for each other. I know it sounds corny, but I always believed he was made for me. That God put us both on this earth so that we could meet. Losing him broke all our hearts, but he's with his beloved God now, and we'll be reunited one day."

"That must be very comforting for you."

"It is. Greg was always thinking about other people. No matter who they were, or what their backgrounds were, or even what their religions were, he wanted to help. He believed everyone could be saved, and I feel like by donating his organs after he'd died, he was still doing it. Still saving people."

Tova's expression crumpled in concern. "Was it something he talked about often? This request for his organs to be used after he was gone."

"We had talked about it, yes, but in that way people do when they don't really believe something is going to happen." She teared up. "I mean, he was still so young, and it happened so suddenly." She clutched her hand to her heart. "But I knew my husband better than anyone and *I* knew what he would have wanted. He was utterly selfless."

"He sounds like a wonderful man," Tova said warmly.

"He really was. The world is a lesser place without him in it."

"This might seem like a strange question," Tova said, "but I assume he donated more than just his liver?"

Clare nodded briskly. "Oh, he did. Everything that could have saved a life was used."

Tova gestured out towards the audience. "So, there are others out there. More people who are walking around with a part of your husband inside them, helping them to live."

"Yes, there are. When I walk down the road and pass strangers in the street, there's always a part of me that wonders if they could be one of the people who'd been lucky enough to be helped by him."

The camera angle changed, focusing on the presenter's face as she stared directly down the lens, addressing the audience at home. "If someone is watching this show today, and they recognise Logan's story and were either recipients of a donor organ around the same sort of time, or perhaps they have a friend or family member who had a transplant around that time, please get in touch with the show. We'd love to make even more reunions happen."

Across the bottom of the screen, a number ran.

Ryan leaned over Shonda to pause it.

"So, the donor seems like the most selfless person ever. A vicar, a family man, and a lifesaving organ donor."

Shonda shrugged. "Some people live their lives that way. They're just naturally good."

"Really? Don't you think everyone has a dark and selfish side?"

"Maybe they do, but some people are better at hiding it than others. I'm not saying it doesn't exist, but they work harder not to give in to that part of themselves. Isn't that what religion is all about? It's not about being perfect, it's about recognising that we're *not* perfect and loving ourselves anyway."

Ryan arched an eyebrow. "*Is* that what religion is about? I thought it was about some mythical being in the sky."

"In part, it is." She wrinkled her nose. "I don't know. I was brought up Christian, but it's not easy to believe when you see the kind of things we do day in, day out."

She had a point.

Ryan refocused on the case. "What have we learned about Logan from the show? Anything that might help us?"

"He doesn't look like someone who's got themselves caught up in something gang-related or anything like that," Shonda said. "Someone who's in trouble, whether that's drugs or money, or debt, wouldn't normally put themselves out there like he did. He seemed to genuinely want to make a connection with his donor's family."

"I agree. He came across as a clean-cut, open young man. I can't see any obvious reason why someone would want him dead."

"Is it worth us talking to the donor's family?" she suggested. "Do they even know he's dead?"

Ryan let out a sigh. "How are they going to take it? It's not a nice thing to hear so soon after losing a husband and father."

"No, but maybe Logan said something to them that might help us."

"Okay, can I leave that with you to break the news and interview them? I think my time will be better spent speaking with Tova Lane. Let's run her for warrants and prior arrests. See if there's anything we should know about before we interview her."

Shonda got to her feet. "Whatever you need, boss."

# Chapter Sixteen

Tova took a sip of her third coffee of the day—black and sugar-free. Being on television added ten pounds, and sweetened lattes were a sure-fire way of making those ten pounds look like twenty.

They'd had numerous call-ins referring to the show she'd done on the transplant donor reunion. Unfortunately, with anything like that, it also encouraged plenty of kooks. People wanted to be on television, no matter what. That was why there were so many reality shows out there now, even when they promised only humiliation and heartbreak to the contestants. People still put themselves up for it, hoping they'd end up famous. She hoped she'd never end up desperate enough to put herself through something like that.

She went through the files her production team had put together for her. They'd whittled down all the nutcases to a few more promising names and faces. Of course, they'd have to send in proof of having received a transplant around the same time as the donor had died, and then have their anonymity waived by the hospital to confirm it, before they'd be brought on the show. She didn't need some know-it-all accusing her of making up guests in order to create a story. Anyway, she took her job seriously and wanted for everything to be correct.

A knock came at her office door, and one of the runners poked their head through. "Umm...Ms Lane... The police are here to talk to you."

Tova frowned. "They are?"

"Yes, shall I bring them through? They're waiting at reception."

Tova got to her feet. "No, don't worry. I'll come out."

That the police had made a personal visit surprised her. She'd reported the graffiti but hadn't mentioned anything about the card since it hadn't actually contained any kind of threat. The police officers must have recognised her name on the report and decided to use it as an excuse to come and meet her. Her chest swelled with pride. People did things like that. She often noticed in restaurants that waiters would change mid-meal, just so they'd each get a turn to serve her table and maybe ask for an autograph. She didn't mind in the slightest—she wouldn't be anyone without her fans—but she'd never considered it might work in her favour with the police as well.

She checked her reflection quickly, fluffing her hair and making sure her makeup hadn't smudged beneath her eyes, then she left her office-stroke-changing room and made her way out to the reception area.

The two police officers, despite being in plain clothes, looked completely out of place. It was a man and woman, and the man in particular caught her attention. She found herself straightening her shoulders and sucking in her non-existent stomach.

*Well, hello, Mr Tall Dark and Handsome.*

She thought he was about her age, maybe a little older. The woman at his side was a good decade younger and had a slightly alternative vibe to her, despite the suit. Her fringe was cut too short, and she had holes in her ears that didn't have any jewellery in.

They spotted her approaching, and so she flashed her widest smile at them both.

"Hi, I'm Tova Lane." She stopped in front of them. "I've got to say, I'm surprised that you came out. I was expecting a crime number sent in the post, not a personal visit."

These weren't just beat officers either, clearly, or they would have been in uniform instead of suits.

The man's brow furrowed. "I'm sorry?"

"Well, something like a car being graffitied doesn't normally warrant a personal visit, does it, but I'm glad you're here. There's something else I need to talk to you about. I wasn't going to mention anything, but it seems silly not to now."

He checked his notebook. "Ms Lane, are you referring to the damage to your car that reported?"

"Yes, of course. Why else would you be here?"

The police officers exchanged a glance.

"Do you have somewhere we can talk?" the female officer said. "In private."

Tova became aware of other members of the production team glancing over at them. Her director, Emmett, was frowning. Suddenly, the floor seemed to shift beneath her feet.

She'd read this wrong.

Tova winced. "You aren't here about the car, are you?"

The woman officer shook her head slowly. "No, we're not. Like I said, if you have somewhere more private we can talk...?"

"Of course. Come this way."

Her cheeks heated, and she turned away to lead them back the way she'd come, using it as an excuse to hide her face from them. Why had she thought so much of herself? Of course they weren't using the bloody car as an excuse to meet her in person. They were busy people. There was something more serious going on.

She led them to her small, windowless dressing room, and closed the door behind them. She'd recovered herself on the short walk and pasted her professional face back on. The bright-blue eyes of the man seemed to drill right through her, and she felt as though she was shrinking. She didn't think she'd get away with bullshitting him, whatever this was about.

"I'm sorry, but I don't think I caught your names," she said.

He pulled ID from the inside of his jacket pocket and flashed it to her. "I'm DI Chase, and this is DS Lawson. We need to ask you some questions about Logan Foss."

She hadn't been expecting to hear that name. "Logan Foss? What about him?"

"You remember him then?"

"Yes, of course. We met on a number of occasions to make an episode of my investigative series, *Tova's Questions*. Is he okay? Did something happen?"

"He's dead, Ms Lane."

She caught her breath. "Dead? Because of the transplant?"

"It may be connected, but that's not what killed him. We're currently treating his death as a murder investigation."

She put her hand to her mouth. "My God, that's awful." Right away, she knew exactly what case they were talking about. If she'd been working on her old job, she'd have been one of the reporters up at the scene trying to get the story. "Was Logan the body found at the warehouse?" She gave her head a slight shake. "I never even considered that it might be him. There are a lot of young men in Bristol. Do you know who killed him?"

"It's an ongoing investigation," DI Chase said. "We've only recently ID'd his body, so we're looking into what kind of person Logan Foss was, and obviously we couldn't have missed that he was recently on your television show."

"Well, yes, he was. He was fine then."

She could have kicked herself for saying that. What a stupid comment. Of course he'd been fine then.

"How did he seem?" he asked. "I mean, outside of how he was on-screen. Did he ever seem nervous or worried about anything?"

"I mean, he was nervous, but most people are right before they appear on television. We're not live, but we do film in front of a live audience consisting of several hundred people, and that's a lot for most people to deal with."

He gestured to her. "You're a reporter, so you interviewed him—which is something we'd have loved to be able to do for our victims. Was there anything you spoke about that didn't make it onto the show?"

"Not really. We talked about how he should handle the additional attention the show would bring him, especially on social media, as the trolls like to jump on our guests, no matter how touching the story is. I could bring the most innocent of people onto the show and there would still be arseholes out there who would want to tear them apart." She shook her head in disgust.

"What about after the show had aired? Did he ever get back in touch with you or the producers? Perhaps he was dealing with one of these trolls?"

"No, he didn't contact me." Something dawned on her, and she widened her eyes. "You don't think him being on the show has anything to do with him being killed, do you?"

"We're simply exploring all possibilities, Ms Lane. Someone wanted Logan dead, and we're just trying to figure out who."

Ice water suddenly trickled through her veins, and she felt the blood drain from her face.

DI Chase must have noticed the change. "Is everything all right, Ms Lane? Did you remember something about Logan?"

She pressed her knuckles to her lips. "No-it-it's probably nothing."

The woman detective spoke gently. "Whatever it is, we'd like to hear it."

Tova blew out a breath and tried not to let her voice tremble. "You remember when I first saw you, I thought you were here for something else?"

"Yes, damage to your car."

"That's right. Someone graffitied it the other day. They wrote the words 'who's next' across the side. And then last night I got home to find someone had left a thank-you card on my front doorstep, and inside was written the same thing. I mean 'who's next?' Are they talking about who to kill next? I put Logan on my TV show. Is that how they chose him? Am I helping a killer pick out his victims?"

She thought to the woman she'd interviewed the other day, Anna. Was *she* going to be next? "You have to warn a woman called Anna Farnham. Her episode goes out tonight. What if the killer goes after her next?"

DI Chase put up a hand to stop her, and she realised she'd been babbling.

"Ms Lane, I appreciate your concern, but I do think you're jumping to conclusions at this point. I'm not saying the two things aren't connected, but we have to look at all possibilities, and this is simply one of them. It could be that whoever killed Logan didn't even know him, and he was just in the wrong place at the wrong time."

"It's got to be more than a coincidence, hasn't it? That someone would leave me those messages and for Logan to be murdered?"

"Coincidences do happen," DS Lawson assured her.

"If Anna ends up murdered and you haven't done anything about it, you'll only have yourself to blame."

She knew she was coming across as dramatic, but she couldn't seem to help herself.

DI Chase's lips thinned, and he appeared to be thinking.

"Do you have the card you were sent? I'll run it for prints, see if anything comes up."

Her heart lifted with hope. Finally, someone was taking her seriously. "You'd do that?"

"Of course. It might be an important piece of evidence."

She went to her handbag and fished it out and gave it to him.

"Ah," he said, before taking out a glove and a clear plastic bag from his pocket. "Just let me..."

Her stomach dropped. "I should have put it in a bag or something, shouldn't I? Damn it. I thought I knew better than that."

"The card has been inside the envelope," he assured her kindly. "That'll hopefully have been enough to protect it."

"Okay, thanks. I hope so."

"Is there any possibility this card came from someone you know, and you've just made a connection where there isn't one?" he asked.

She shook her head. "Why wouldn't they sign their name?"

"Perhaps they assumed you'd know who it was from?"

"Yes, and I do. The same person who wrote the same words across my car." She thought of something. "I can send you photographs of the car, too."

"Is the car here?"

"No, it's in the garage having the paintwork repaired. It never occurred to me that it might be evidence for something—certainly not evidence in a murder case."

The possibility that whoever did that to her car might have also killed Logan Foss terrified her. Not only that, if it was the same person, they also knew where she lived.

DI Chase linked his fingers together. "I'm going to need the name of the garage working on your vehicle. With any luck, they won't have started repainting it yet. I'll get forensics to see if they can get any evidence. Even if the car has been repainted, we still might be able to get fingerprints. We'll need to take your prints, too, so we can rule them out of the investigation."

"No problem." Tova sniffed and jotted down the name of the garage and handed it over. "Thank you."

"We don't yet know that this is connected to the case, Ms Lane," he assured her. "You must understand that you're a public figure, and I'm sure this isn't the first time you've received strange post or had unsettling things happen."

"Well, no, it isn't," she admitted, heat rising to her face.

There was one time a fan kept sending her pairs of skimpy lace thongs in the post, telling her to wear them for the day and then send them back to him. Because the man was stupid enough to include a stamped addressed return envelope, it was easy enough to get the police to show up at his door and give him a warning, but that hadn't stopped him. The underwear kept turning up. He must have got bored eventually or moved on to some other poor woman. The amount of abuse she got online was ridiculous, too, especially after she'd made a programme that was in some way 'anti-men' such as the one she'd most recently filmed with Anna Farnham. Those kinds of shows were bound to trigger all the trolls.

She took a breath before she tried to explain. "I think it's that this feels so much closer to home—and I mean that literally as well as figuratively. Whoever left that card knows where I live, and whoever graffitied my car made it right beneath my work. Now you're telling me a man I interviewed not so long ago is dead. You can't blame me for being spooked."

"Not at all. It's completely understandable. Do you live alone?"

"Yes, I do."

"Have you got anyone who can come and stay with you for a few days, or maybe you could go and stay with a family member or friend?"

"The only family I've got is my grandmother, and she's in her nineties and lives in a home. I wouldn't feel like I could impose on a friend."

What friends did she even have? No real ones, it felt like. Just acquaintances. She suddenly felt completely alone and strangely close to tears.

DI Chase took a card from the inside of his pocket and handed it to her. "If anything else happens, or you think of something Logan Foss might have said that you didn't already mention, my number is on there."

She sniffed. "Okay, thank you."

Tova waited until the police had left and then closed the door of her dressing room. The strength left her legs, and she slumped into her chair and put her head in her hands. Poor Logan Foss was dead. He'd been such a decent kind of bloke as well—too young for her—but with so much potential. What kind of person murdered someone who had already been through so much? Was it the same kind of person who would leave her strange notes? Could she convince herself these two things weren't connected? Maybe she should go and stay in a hotel, though there didn't seem to be much point since whoever had left the notes knew where she worked.

Whatever she decided to do, she knew she needed to warn those around her. If someone else was killed because they'd done her the grace of appearing on her show, she'd never forgive herself.

# Chapter Seventeen

Ryan and Mallory grabbed something to eat on the way back into the office. They ate in the car with the engine still running, delaying the inevitable return to the bustle of the workplace.

Mallory took a big bite of her cheese and onion sandwich.

Ryan turned up his nose at her choice of filling. "Your breath is going to stink after that."

She deliberately blew in his direction and then laughed at his expression. "Good thing the only person who gets to sit so close to me is you."

"What about the boyfriend?"

"If you're talking about Daniel, then no? I think I put a nail in that coffin last night when I accused him of interrogating Oliver."

He twisted in his seat to face her. "Why did you do that?"

"Oh, I don't know. It doesn't matter. I don't have time for anyone else anyway." She switched topics. "What did you make of Tova Lane then?"

"She wasn't what I expected. I mean, she was in some ways. She's beautiful, in that slightly frozen way that comes from a decent dose of Botox and too much makeup. But I'd expected her to be interested in the story, since she's a reporter, but she seemed more frightened than anything else."

Mallory pursed her lips. "You don't really think the thing about her car, and then that card, could be connected to Logan's murder?"

"Most likely not, but there is a chance someone saw the show and took a disliking to him."

"Enough to murder him and steal his liver?"

He shrugged. "Possibly. What would you do with another person's liver?"

"Me, personally?" she asked with an arched brow.

"You know what I mean."

"Sell it is the most obvious answer. The black market organ trade is big business."

"But the pathologist ruled that out, so let's think outside the box. What about some not-so-obvious answers."

She grimaced. "Eat it? Maybe there's a black market trade for human offal as well? People who have a taste for cannibalism—no pun intended."

"You think someone might have gone all Hannibal Lecter on us? Human liver and fava beans?"

"And don't forget the nice chianti," she retorted.

"Maybe they didn't even sell it. Maybe they just wanted it for that reason themselves?"

Mallory pulled another face. "You really think we're dealing with a cannibal right here in Bristol? Isn't it more likely that whoever did this is simply a psychopath?"

"There's always a reason, even if it's only in the killer's head and we don't understand it. I remember a case where a woman cut open her baby's stomach because she believed there was a snake living inside him. To us, her reasoning didn't make any sense, but in her mind, the baby was in danger, and she needed to save him. It was completely real."

Mallory shook her head. "Jesus, poor kid."

"He survived," Ryan said. "The father suspected the mother was very unwell and burst in on her just after she'd done it. His quick actions and calling an ambulance and the police saved his son's life."

"Even so, imagine going through your life knowing that your own mother did that to you. It would be hard to deal with."

"Yes, it would." He turned his thoughts back to his current case. "Maybe we're looking at some kind of strange religious ritual, or someone who is seriously mentally ill. Let's check to see if there's any record of someone who's committed a crime and harvested an organ in the past. Maybe they've been recently released from a mental facility."

Mallory nodded. "Makes sense."

He finished what remained of his chicken and salad sandwich and started the car. "We'd better get back to the office, see if anyone else has made any progress."

RYAN GATHERED HIS TEAM together and brought them up to speed with what they'd learned about Logan being on Tova Lane's show.

"*Tova's Questions* gets hundreds of thousands of viewers," he said. "If there's a chance his murder is connected to him being on that show, it doesn't help us narrow things down any. They do film in front of a live audience, and so I've requested the list of who was there that day, just to see if any names jump out, but again, we're looking at hundreds of people."

Finding out about the show had made their job harder instead of easier. Ryan focused on the actions he'd given his constables. Those leads were tangible—things they could actually work with.

"Craig," he said to DC Penn, "how did you get on at the sport's shop where Logan worked?"

"I spoke to his co-workers, but they all said that nothing out of the ordinary happened that day. Logan acted the same as ever. He kept his head down and got on with his work. He didn't seem like anything in particular was troubling him."

"What did his colleagues make of him in general?"

"He seemed to be liked, but they all said they didn't know him that well. They were all youngsters, late teens and early twenties. They said that Logan kept himself to himself and doesn't drink, so he never joined them on nights out, which I guess is where they do most of their bonding at that age."

DC Craig Penn wasn't much older than the twenty-somethings he was talking about but spoke about them as though they were a different category altogether.

Ryan thought for a moment. "That must have been hard for him, seeing others his age having fun but not being able to join in."

"Yeah, poor bloke had a tough life. It's fucking shit that it ended like that."

Ryan agreed. "What else have we got?" he asked the rest of his team.

DC Dev Kharral jumped in. "I spoke to the neighbours but didn't get anywhere. No one heard or saw anything."

"That surprises me," Ryan said. "At that time in the evening, people must have been in, back from work and not yet out for the night. If he lived in a flat, he must have had people close by."

"He did, but like I said, no one saw or heard anything."

Ryan frowned. "If he was taken against his will, surely he would have fought back or at least shouted out. Someone would have seen or heard something."

Dev lifted both hands. "Maybe he didn't go against his will."

"Good point. So he might have known whoever took him and went with them willingly."

"Or it was someone like a police officer who didn't give him much choice."

Ryan could see Dev's point of view, but it always jarred with him to hear of the possibility of police involvement in a crime. He liked to think of them as the good guys, but he also knew they were only human and made mistakes. There was a big difference between making a mistake and deliberately abducting someone for murder, however.

Perhaps seeing his boss's expression, Dev added, "Or someone posing as the police."

Ryan considered this for a moment.

Another of his DCs stepped in. "I've made some progress with the security footage between his place of work and his flat," Linda said. "Logan was caught on a security camera in the local Tesco Metro buying a microwave curry. That was at six-thirteen the night that he died, so we know he was still alive then."

"Do we know if a curry was found at his flat or in his stomach during the post-mortem report?"

Mallory pressed her lips together. "There was no mention of a recently eaten meal during the post-mortem report. I'm not sure about the flat."

"We need to find out." He thought for a moment. "Actually, I'm going to go down there, take a look for myself."

"I'll come," Mallory said. "Unless you've got somewhere else you need me to be?"

"Nope. Some company sounds good."

THE ROAD OUTSIDE LOGAN Foss's flat was busy with police presence. Search teams worked along the street, analysing every tossed cigarette butt or empty Coke can for possible evidence. Cordon tape blocked off the road, and a second, inner cordon, sealed off the entrance to the flat.

Ryan wasn't able to see Logan's front door from his position on the road. He had to walk between the two buildings to where it was located on the side of the house.

"If Logan was taken from the flat," he said to Mallory, "was he brought out here, onto the road, in full view of the neighbours, or is there rear access?"

Mallory checked her notes. "As far as I'm aware, there's only a garden at the rear. It backs onto another garden, so I wouldn't imagine they'd have gone that way."

"If Logan had been struggling or fighting whoever attacked him, wouldn't he have been seen? Or if he'd been unconscious, someone must have noticed him being dragged out of the flat and put in a car or van?"

"If it happened after work, it would have been dark," Mallory pointed out.

Ryan observed the streetlights positioned at regular intervals. "But it would have been well-lit, nevertheless. Let's check with the council and make sure all the lights were working the night Logan was killed."

She nodded and jotted it down.

"Of course, if Logan knew his attacker and went with them willingly, it would explain why no one heard any shouting or saw a struggle. It simply didn't catch anyone's attention."

Mallory nipped at a piece of dry skin on her lower lip. "But why leave the phone and door unlocked?"

"Could he have been in a rush? Had whoever taken him made it sound like there was an emergency with something?"

He thought to what DC Kharral had suggested about it being a police officer or someone posing as one. Would Logan have left his phone and keys behind if he thought he was being arrested?

Mallory exhaled. "Maybe. Or he simply didn't think he was going to be gone for long. I mean, if someone wanted me to see something right outside my house, I wouldn't bother grabbing my phone or locking up behind me either."

He nodded in agreement. "Good point. Let's go and take a look around."

Ryan pulled on some gloves and booties, flashed his ID at the uniformed officer guarding the inner cordon, signed the log, and then ducked beneath the tape. He walked down the short path to the front door, Mallory close behind. A small canopy above it offered shelter from the rain when it was wet. Ryan paused again and took in his surroundings. The house next door didn't have any windows that looked directly down onto the path. There was a security light beside the door—did it come on with motion? He needed to check. He already knew there weren't any security cameras around, but he still couldn't help making sure for himself.

Satisfied there weren't, he entered the flat. The place was small and already felt cramped with him and Mallory both entering. The kitchen and living room were all set in the same area, a breakfast bar dividing the kitchen from the living space.

Mallory gestured to the breakfast bar. "This was where his keys were found, together with his phone."

He took in the rest of the flat. There was nothing about it that set off any alarm bells. He remembered how Logan had been caught on CCTV buying a curry, but that the post-mortem hadn't reported any sign of it in his stomach.

Ryan went to the fridge and opened it. Sure enough, there was a Tesco red Thai curry microwave meal.

"He didn't have time to eat then," he mused. "Whoever took him arrived before he'd had the chance to have dinner."

Mallory shrugged. "Or he bought the curry for a different night."

Ryan held the fridge door open wider. "Does it look as though Logan was a meal planner?"

The interior was practically bare.

"That helps us narrow down the time he was taken then," she said. "What time do people who work regular jobs eat dinner at? Surely he wouldn't eat much later than eight? So, if he was taken or left willingly, it would be between six-thirty and eight."

Ryan nodded. "And we know he hadn't been dead long when his body was found, so that would fit in the with the timescale. Let's get footage from all the traffic cameras around this area for that time. With any luck, we'll catch Logan Foss sitting in the passenger seat of the car belonging to whoever took him."

# Chapter Eighteen

It hadn't been an easy thing for Macie to do, but in the end, she'd decided her parents were right and she'd handwritten a letter to her donor's family, folded the piece of paper in half, slipped it into an envelope, and taken it herself to the donor centre. There, it would be passed on to the donor's family—if they wanted to hear from her. There was a good possibility that they wanted to stay anonymous as well, and Macie would never hear back. She wasn't sure how she felt about that. On one hand, she would be relieved not to feel as though she was going to let them down, that she wouldn't have to go through the experience of them wishing something as important as their loved one's heart had gone to someone else. But on the other hand, it would be like a rejection of sorts, and she'd have to move forward with the knowledge that they didn't want to know her.

Her phone buzzed with a notification, and she picked it up and swiped the screen. It was a message via Instagram.

*Hi, Macie. Sorry to message you out of the blue. I'm a researcher for Tova's Questions, and I came across your social media account. I'm looking into receivers of organs for the family of a man who died and donated his organs, and your timeline and location fits the profile. We would need to confirm the match via the donor centre, but if you're willing to do that, and it's a match, the family of your donor would really love to meet you.*

*We'd love to talk about doing the reunion on our show. However, if this isn't something you're interested in and would prefer to keep your anonymity, then we completely respect that. Hope to hear from you. Diana.*

Macie sucked in a breath and read the message over again. Her donor's family wanted to meet her? And on a television programme? Did that mean they'd also contacted the donor centre and she'd hear from them soon?

She knew exactly what show the researcher was referring to—she'd seen the last episode, of course she had. It had been so close to home, and she had to admit that it had been touching. So much of it had resonated with her, and she'd watched with tears in her eyes. A part of her had even been tempted to reach out to Logan Foss and tell him that she suspected she was also one of the people who'd received the gift of a new chance at life from the same donor, but she never had.

She continued to stare at the message. What should she do? Was that something she wanted to get involved with? She remembered all the posts she'd made where she'd felt as though she'd revealed too much about herself and how she'd deleted them. If she took part in this show, she wouldn't be able to delete what she didn't like. It would be out there forever.

The thought of meeting her donor's family made her uncomfortable, too. Even though she'd written the letter, it was very different communicating with someone in writing than doing so face to face and on television. What if they could see right through her? They might be able to see how she was wasting her opportunity and then they'd hate her for it.

But maybe it would be like ripping off a plaster? She could get it done and not have to sit in wait for a reply to her letter.

It might even be that this wasn't her donor's family, and they had the wrong person, in which case she wouldn't have lost anything.

Macie swiped her thumb across the screen again and hit 'reply'.

# Chapter Nineteen

Tova knocked on her director's door.

Her stomach was in knots, and she hadn't been able to get the visit from the police out of her head. Everything felt wrong, off kilter, as though she was just waiting for something terrible to happen. No, something terrible already *had* happened. Poor Logan Foss was dead. Murdered. And it might have had something to do with her show.

Did that mean, unwittingly, she was to blame?

Emmett's voice came from inside, and she cracked open the door.

"Tova," he said, "what can I do for you?"

Emmett's office was far nicer than hers, and a wave of jealously went through her. She often thought she was the most important part of her show—after all, it was named after her—but then she saw how crappy her office was compared with Emmett's and thought they would can her the minute her ratings started to drop.

She slipped inside and closed the door behind her. "The police were here. You remember Logan Foss from the transplant reunion show?"

"Of course."

"He was found murdered."

Emmett's eyes widened. "Jesus Christ. By whom?"

"The police don't know yet. The strange thing is that it happened the night before someone wrote 'who's next' on my car and then sent me a thank-you card saying the same thing. I can't help feeling as though they're connected."

He frowned. "What are you saying? That whoever killed Logan sent you those messages?"

"It's a possibility, yes, and the police are taking it seriously, too. They've taken the card in to be analysed for fingerprints."

He rubbed his mouth with his fingers. "Well, this could make for an interesting episode, don't you think?" He held his hands up and drew a rectangle with them in the air. "From stalker to killer. When fans go too far."

The suggestion shocked her. "No, that wasn't where I was going with this at all!"

It had crossed her mind, though, hadn't it? This was going to pull the viewers in like nothing else. Even if those notes had nothing to do with what had happened to Logan, just the fact one of her ex-guests had been murdered made a good story. As would getting the reaction from the donor's family. How did it feel to them? Was it like losing their loved one all over again?

He waggled a finger at her. "I recognise that face, Tova. The old cogs are working."

She forced herself to back up. "That wasn't what I was trying to say at all. In fact, I think we should go the other way and put a pause on the show. We could say it was a sign of respect."

"Have you lost your mind, Tova? We can't do that."

"Why not?"

He flung out both hands. "Because the show must go on, as they say. If you want to do a memorial for Logan Foss, we'll do a live special and dedicate the next show to him. The audience will like that."

"But what about the guests? If someone is stalking me and killing them, we could be putting them in danger by airing the next episode."

"If," he said. "That's a pretty important word in that sentence. And it's a big 'if', too. We don't have any proof that what you're describing is anything more than your overactive imagination."

Her jaw dropped. "I didn't imagine the card or the graffiti on my car, and I certainly didn't imagine Logan Foss being murdered!"

"No, but you might be seeing connections where there aren't any."

"That's not what the police said," she half-lied, "and, no offence, but I think I'll put their opinion above yours on this one."

He hardened his tone. "You can put my opinion wherever you want, but I'm not cancelling the show, and if you even consider doing something to screw it up, I'll make sure you're sued for breaching your contract, is that understood, Tova? You don't want to create a reputation for yourself as a troublemaker in this business. No one will want to work with you again. You're not so big as to stop yourself becoming a nobody."

The worst part was that he was completely right.

"We need to push ahead," he continued. "Where are we with finding the next star of our show? I wanted to do a follow-up with the donor's family, remember. It'll be even sweeter now that Logan Foss is dead. Finding this new part of their loved one still alive will be like we're helping them to heal all over again."

It felt completely exploitative of the poor family. Not only had they lost their husband and father, but they were now going to find out that the young man who'd been the recipient of their loved one's liver had been brutally murdered.

"They might not want to come back on the show after hearing that," Tova suggested.

Emmett snorted. "You met the donor's wife, Clare, and how she gushed about her husband the entire time. She loved the whole experience, all that attention and being in the limelight. I bet she'll just use this as another way to get noticed."

"That's really harsh, Emmett. She lost the man she loved. You of all people should understand how that feels. Have a heart."

He waved her away. "I have a heart."

"No, you've grown hard. I know it's been difficult for you lately—"

"I'm not going down that road, Tova."

Emmett had taken some time off a few months back. Personal issues, they'd been told. Lost someone he loved—a close friend, apparently, but she thought it was a little more.

He wasn't particularly camp, and she never would have known unless he'd told her. Not that it bothered Tova in the slightest. Love was love in her mind, and whoever people dated was none of her business. She wished her love life was as torrid. Maybe she should switch to dating women and see if that improved her chances of ever settling down.

She sighed. "So you're saying nothing has changed?"

"Not a thing, Tova. Now get back to work. I want to get the donor family back into the studio as soon as possible. Strike while the iron's hot."

"And the show featuring Anna Farnham is still going out tonight?"

"Right on schedule," he said.

Tova nodded and left the office. She paused in the corridor outside and chewed at her lower lip. What if she was right and someone was killing off her guests? If Anna's show went out tonight, wouldn't that mean Anna was in danger? She had to contact her, she decided.

She went back to her dressing room, opened her laptop, and pulled up her guest files. She located Anna Farnham's name and phone number. She was fairly sure Anna wouldn't be expecting to hear from her.

She dialled the number, and within a couple of rings Anna answered.

"Hello?"

"Anna, hi, it's Tova Lane."

"Tova! What a surprise. Are you calling about the show tonight?"

"Umm, in a way, yes." How the hell was she going to put this without freaking the other woman out? "Something's happened, and I thought you should know."

"Oh?"

"Did you hear about a body of a man being found the other day?"

Anna's tone was cautious. "Yes, I did."

"It was that of Logan Foss, the guest on my previous show."

"My God, I'm so sorry." Anna paused and then said, "What's it got to do with me?"

"Most likely nothing, but not long after the murder I received some strange messages."

"What kind of messages?"

Tova hesitated, realising how ridiculous this sounded. "They asked who was next?"

"Who was next? Do you mean who was next to die?"

"Honestly, I don't know what they mean. I've passed them over to the police, and they're looking into it. But since you're also now connected to the show, I wanted to call you and just ask you to be extra careful. Don't go out on your own if you can help it. Get a taxi to places instead of walking. Make sure your doors and windows are locked at night. That kind of thing."

There was silence on the line, and then Anna said, "How was the other guest killed?"

"I don't know the details, sorry."

"So, I'm just supposed to watch my back?"

"Basically, yes. I didn't want to scare you, but I also didn't want to not say anything and for something to happen. I'd never forgive myself."

"When you warned me about backlash from people online, I never expected an actual murderer to turn up."

"I know, and I'm sorry. The police aren't even sure it's connected yet. There's the chance Logan had a whole other life that we're unaware of and he was killed because of that, or maybe he was simply in the wrong place at the wrong time. We just don't know yet."

A blow of air came down the line. "Okay, I appreciate you letting me know. Will you keep me updated about any developments?"

"Absolutely."

# Chapter Twenty

It had been a long day, and Ryan found himself wanting to see a friendly face. It wasn't too late yet, so he thought he'd stop by Donna's and see how she was doing. They hadn't had a chance to talk since she'd got the all-clear. With any luck, she'd suggest a takeaway and a bottle of wine, and he wouldn't have to spend yet another night alone in his flat.

Ryan drove down her road. He approached her house and signalled to turn onto her driveway, just as a silver Audi ahead of him, facing his direction, pulled away from the curb too quickly. Ryan caught sight of the dark-haired man hunched behind the steering wheel. It had only been a flash, but he still recognised him.

Donna's ex, Tony. At least, her *other* ex. What the fuck was he doing here? Why had he left in such a rush?

Adrenaline surged through him. He was still furious at the way that dickhead had treated Donna. How could someone leave a person they'd claimed to love at the time they were needed the most? Tony was a pathetic excuse for a man, as far as Ryan was concerned, and that had nothing to do with the fact he'd been banging Ryan's ex-wife...okay, only a small amount to do with it. Ryan had played numerous moments over in his head where he'd come face to face with that prick and told him exactly what he thought of him. Ryan knew he was far from faultless concerning how things had gone between him and Donna after their daughter had died, but Tony had no excuses. He was just a selfish prick, end of story, and he had no right creeping around Donna again.

The tail lights of the Audi had vanished around the bend. He wasn't going to chase after him, though it was tempting.

"Fucking knob." His hands tightened around the steering wheel.

He glanced over at the house. A shape moved in the living room window, and the curtain twitched. *Donna*. Had Tony been in to see her? She had definitely seen Ryan now, and it wasn't as though he could just sit here in his car stewing.

Ryan threw open the car door and climbed out.

The front door opened, and Donna lifted her hand in a wave. Her hair hadn't started to grow back yet, and it always felt like a shock to see her naked head. She was still beautiful, even without the hair, perhaps even more so. There was a new kind of vulnerability to her. She'd always been so strong before, even after Hayley died. It was pathetic, but he'd always felt as though she never needed him, that she would cope perfectly well with everything on her own, perhaps even cope better since she didn't have to take his feelings into account.

The way her lips were pinched and her eyes were glassy made him think she hadn't been happy about Tony's appearance here either, and a little part of him unknotted inside. Had he been worried about her ex swanning back in and stealing his thunder?

She let him inside and closed the door behind him.

"You'd better come through," she said, leading him into the lounge.

"Are you okay?" he asked.

Donna blinked too fast, in that way she did when she was trying not to cry. Her voice was overly bright. "Yes, fine. Why?"

"I thought I just saw Dickhead's car driving off."

"Oh, yeah. You did. He just popped in to say hi."

"You get the all-clear and all of a sudden he's crawling all over you again?"

She glanced away. "It's not like that. He's just a friend who was checking up on me."

Ryan raised both eyebrows. "A friend? He's considered a friend now. That son of a bitch scarpered the minute he found out about the cancer. You haven't seen him for months. And now you get to ring the bell and all of a sudden he's back again." Ryan paced back and forth across the room. "The man is a fucking prick. He wasn't there for you through the hard stuff. Remember that."

She put out a hand. "Ryan, stop it. First of all, he only came around to say hi, that's all. Secondly, this isn't any of your business. We're not married anymore, remember? And you don't get to have a say in who I choose to spend time with."

His jaw dropped. "That wasn't what I was trying to do. I came around to see you, only to find you've been crying, and that idiot was here. I'm trying to protect you."

She folded her arms around her torso. "I'm a grown woman who's just beaten cancer. I don't need my ex-husband making decisions about my personal life."

"I didn't realise that was what I was doing."

"Didn't you? Should I invite him back again then?"

"Fucking hell, no way."

She threw up a hand. "See."

"See what? You asked me for my opinion, and I gave it to you."

She sighed in exasperation. "I only asked to back up what I was saying. I know you, Ryan. We were married, remember. You don't have to say something out loud for me to know exactly what you mean. You don't approve of him coming here and think I should tell him not to come back."

His frustration mounted. "And why would that be a bad thing? That wanker ran for the hills the moment you got your diagnosis. Where has he been over the past six months? Holding your hand while you were having chemo? Bringing you food around when you were too weak to make it yourself? He didn't even phone to ask how you were. But the minute you rang the bell with the all-clear, he's creeping around again."

She stared at him for a moment.

"Why have you even been helping me, Ryan? Is it just so you get to have a say in my life again? Do I owe you something now? Is that it?"

"No, of course not."

Why *had* he been helping her? Was it because he'd wanted to be a part of her life again and this had been his way in? No, that wasn't true. He cared about her. She'd been the mother of his child, and they'd been through a lot together. He couldn't have just abandoned her when she'd been in need.

"Maybe I should leave," he said.

"Maybe you should."

He couldn't understand why she was so angry with him. What exactly had he done wrong? The only thing he could think was that he'd said out loud what she had been thinking—that her ex was only paying her attention now because she was better. He was saying what she didn't want to hear, and that meant, deep down, she wanted that dickhead back. She still had feelings for him.

Ryan was surprised at the breadth of pain that caused him. She wanted Tony back, and he had to just stand by and watch.

Abruptly, he turned to the front door. "Take care of yourself, Donna."

"Ryan, don't be like that."

He couldn't bring himself to be in her company. She didn't need him anymore, so he was gone. He dug deeper inside himself, wanting to understand his own motives. He knew himself well enough to admit that he wasn't completely altruistic. Perhaps he wanted to be back in her life. Or perhaps she'd simply been a distraction for him, a way of blocking out everything else?

Or maybe it was simply that he still loved her and couldn't stand to see her hurt.

# Chapter Twenty-One

Ryan went into work the following morning with a headache and a sour mouth. It was rare he drank to extremes—hangovers played havoc with his OCD—but last night he'd been feeling sorry for himself, and he'd hit a bottle of whiskey far harder than was sensible. In fact, he couldn't even remember getting himself to bed. He'd woken up at four a.m. with a full bladder and still dressed, his head pounding. He'd managed to get himself to the bathroom and had downed a couple of paracetamols and taken himself back to bed, but it had been hard getting back to sleep again.

Now he felt like shit, had a busy day ahead of him, and was deeply regretting his life choices.

He checked his phone to make sure he hadn't made any drunk calls or texts to Donna, but it seemed he was in the clear.

What a fucking idiot he was. Could he really still be in love with his ex-wife?

Mallory slid a large coffee onto his desk. "You look like you could use this?"

"That bad, huh?"

"Well, you're not looking good."

He yawned and rubbed at his eyes with the balls of his hands. "Give me an hour or two, and I'll be fine."

"Is everything all right?" she asked, concerned.

He knew it wasn't like him to turn up at work hungover. It wasn't professional at all, and the darkness of self-hatred seeped into his soul.

"Just personal stuff. I'll be fine."

"Okay, but I'm always here if you need to talk." She looked as though she was going to walk away and then remembered something. "Oh, I heard back from SOCO. They went down to the garage that's looking after Tova's car. The car had already been repainted. It's just having the finishing touches done to it. They've picked up some prints, but so far, they match the man who's been working on it. There's a lot of someone else's in the interior, but those are most likely belonging to Tova. We still need to cross reference them."

He realised he'd been absentmindedly straightening the items on his desk when they were already perfectly straight and snatched his hand away. From the small, sympathetic smile on his sergeant's face, she'd seen him do it.

"Anything back about the letter?" he asked.

"Nothing. Whoever wrote and delivered it must have been careful to wear gloves and not leave any fibres."

"Okay, thanks. I'll drink this," he nodded at the coffee, "and then I'll call a briefing."

They were several days into this case now, and they still didn't have a substantial lead. He'd been sure the CCTV from around Logan's flat would have brought up something by now, but so far, they'd had no such luck. With no substantial witnesses either, he was starting to worry whoever had killed Logan Foss was going to get away with it.

Ryan called the briefing. His DCI sat in on it as well. He did his roll call for the morning and hoped his boss didn't notice he was hungover.

Dev stood.

"I thought you should know that we got the report back from Digital Forensics on Logan's phone. We already know the phone's final location because it was left at the flat, but he last used it the morning he died to call his manager at work. We checked with the manager, and he said Logan had called him to double-check his shift start time."

"What about messages or social media," Ryan asked. "Anything to report?"

"Yes, unfortunately, it's not a pretty picture. You need to take a look at the messages he'd been receiving via social media."

Dev used the smart board on the wall to bring up screenshots of some of the messages that had been sent to Logan.

*You should have died on the table.*

*What a waste of a good liver.*

*You sound like a loser.*

*It's sick to walk around with a piece of someone else inside you. What a freak.*

"Jesus Christ." Ryan shook his head in disbelief. "How can someone who's had a liver transplant inspire such hatred? He had life-saving surgery. What is there to hate?"

Dev shrugged. "People still came up with plenty of reasons to troll him."

"What was his reaction? Has he replied to any of them?"

"Amazingly, no, he hasn't." Dev paused, then added, "I'm not sure I'd be quite that strong-willed."

"No, me neither," Ryan agreed. "Maybe he didn't even read them. Just because they've been posted doesn't mean Logan paid any attention to them."

Mallory spoke up from her seat. "Is it possible one of these people is the one responsible for killing him? Could they hate him so much that online trolling wasn't enough, and they took it a step further?"

Ryan considered it. "If they were so offended by him being a transplant recipient, would that be enough of a motive to cut his liver out of him?"

"I'm not sure," Dev said. "These people tend to be cowards. They use the anonymity of the internet to hide behind. Is that the same kind of person who would come to Logan's home?"

"Predators use the internet to lure people in all the time," Mallory pointed out.

Dev jabbed his finger her way. "But if we're considering that Logan knew whoever took him, it wouldn't fit the profile of them being an anonymous troll on the internet."

Ryan ran his hand over his face and let out a sigh. "Okay, this is going to be pretty time-consuming, but we're going to need to put some more manpower into going through each of these comments and messages and seeing if there's anything that jumps out as being more than just some online trolling. Did he exchange any messages where he might have given an idea about his address? How easy is it to find out where he lives online?"

"They didn't need to find out where he lives online," Mallory said. "If they found out where he works, they could have simply followed him home."

"Good point. Let's get back onto the CCTV. Is there anyone suspicious hanging around the same time Logan went into the shop? What about the CCTV cameras at his place of work? They might have caught someone lurking around outside, waiting for him to leave."

"We'll go over them again, boss," Craig said. "We might have missed something the first time round."

"Good." Ryan summarised what they knew. "It takes fifteen minutes to walk between the Tesco Metro from his flat, and we know Logan made it home, because we found the curry in the fridge, so let's assume he got back around six-thirty. His body was discovered here," he stabbed his finger at the spot on the map, "at the warehouse at ten-thirty. We know he'd already been dead for at a couple of hours when his body was found, so we're really starting to narrow things down now. That gives only a two-hour window for Logan to have been snatched—or possibly left willingly—and driven the twenty-five minutes to the warehouse, where he was killed and his liver removed.

"We know Logan lost a trainer before he got to the warehouse, which hints at a struggle, though there's no sign of blood or any kind of violence happening at his flat. The trainer still hasn't shown up, so where did Logan lose it? In his kidnapper's car? He didn't walk from the car to the warehouse as the sock he was wearing was clean." His mind was on a roll. Sometimes he felt as though he was watching a film playing out in his head, with each of the pieces dropping into place as events unravelled.

"Whoever killed Logan must have knocked him unconscious by a blow to the back of the head in the car or van they used and then carried him into the warehouse. We know from the shoeprint that was found in the blood that the killer wears a size ten, and from that we can guess he's approximately six feet tall. Logan Foss wasn't a small man either, so we must be looking for someone physically strong, either in a position of authority, or someone who was already known to the victim. I don't think we can rule out the possibility that this might have even been the work of two people. This was planned. They'd checked out the location of the warehouse before. They must have used a vehicle of some kind to get Logan to the warehouse. We have a time zone of somewhere between six-thirty and eight where he drove Logan between Logan's flat and the warehouse. What's the most likely route they took? I want every CCTV camera from each variation of those routes checked between those times. There's no way we haven't caught the vehicle on at least one camera."

"That's still going to be a lot of vehicles, boss," Dev said, tapping the end of his pen against his lips. "You want all of them checked?"

"You got it."

All the hate messages Logan Foss had received played on his mind. Ryan wondered if the other people on the show received similar hate messages.

"Has anyone talked to the family yet?" he said.

"Foss's family?" Mallory checked.

"No, the donor's family. The ones who appeared on the show with Logan."

"I did, boss," Shonda said. "Remember?"

He gave his head a slight shake. "Yes, of course. How did you get on?"

"Clare McIver, the donor's wife, was upset to hear about Logan's murder, but she didn't have any information about him that we didn't already know."

Ryan thought for a moment. While he trusted his team, sometimes he wanted to get in front of people himself to really understand what they were about.

"Okay, thanks. With this new information, I think I'll pop round and have a chat with her about the trolling, see if there was anything the family experienced that they didn't think to tell us about before."

"YOU'LL HAVE TO EXCUSE the mess," Clare McIver said as she let Ryan and Mallory into her three-bedroom, semi-detached home. "We haven't been in here long. We were in a parish house before this one, but obviously, with my husband dead, we no longer qualified for that."

"You had to move? That seems harsh."

"It was expected. The new vicar's family needed the house."

"I see."

"Can I get you anything?" she said as she led them through into the kitchen. "I can put the kettle on, if you'd like?"

"We're fine, but thank you."

"Well, come in and sit down."

She gestured at the kitchen table, and Ryan and Mallory took seats, side by side.

Surreptitiously, Ryan took in the décor. In pride of place, on the wall beside the table, was a large crucifix. Just across from that was a painted picture of Jesus Christ. Ryan respected that some people found a comfort in religion, but this was a bit much for him. He felt judged just by being in the room. He'd already known that this was a religious home—after all, her husband had been a vicar—but, even then, it was overwhelming. Where most people would have pictures of their children, she had the last supper and Mary gazing down at a baby Jesus.

Clare took a seat opposite.

She put her hand to her chest. "Can I just start by saying that it broke my heart to hear of Logan. It felt a bit like we were losing my husband all over again, even though I know that wasn't the case. But another piece of him had died, do you understand? And that hurt."

"I'm very sorry for the loss of your husband, Gregory," Mallory said. "He sounded like a good man."

"He really was. The best. I miss him with all my heart. That he was at least able to help others when he passed gave us some comfort, though, as was the fact God wanted him by His side."

Ryan tried to ignore the last comment. "You went on Tova Lane's show to find Logan Foss?"

"That's right. I know it seems like a crazy thing to do, but I was watching the television one night, and her show came on, and at the end there was a call out for stories and asking people to get in touch with the production team. I had a moment of madness and called in. It was like even through the grief, there was hope, and I wanted to share that with people. Then when I spoke to the production team and they suggested that they reached out to the people who had received his organs, it just felt perfect. I wrote a letter to the transplant centre, and the production company put calls out on social media and on the show asking for people to get in touch if they happened to receive a transplant at the same time Greg died, and sure enough, Logan came forward."

"Do you mind me asking how your husband died?" Ryan said.

"Car accident," she replied. "It was all so sudden. Luckily, no one else was hurt, which is a blessing from Heaven, but it broke all our hearts to lose him so suddenly."

He offered her a sympathetic smile. "It must have been hard for the children as well."

"It was. We were lucky to have been able to say goodbye to Greg in the hospital, so at least we got some closure, and of course, meeting Logan was a blessing, too. It breaks my heart that someone would do such a thing to him, but I hope both he and Greg are meeting in Heaven now."

"You said he was in car accident?" Ryan pressed on. "What happened?"

"He lost control of it. Simple as that. The weather was bad—black ice on the road—and he was going a little too fast. He hit a patch and skidded off the road and wrapped the car around a tree. The police investigated and said it was nothing more than a tragic accident." She crossed herself and looked to the ceiling. "God wanted His angel back."

Ryan and Mallory exchanged glances. It was good she took comfort in her religion, but it made them both a little uncomfortable.

Ryan cleared his throat. "How long after the accident was it deemed that he wouldn't make a recovery?"

"Within hours. The doctors determined he had no brain activity. It was very hard. We thought it was better that some good came out of his death."

"We?"

"Me and the children. They were in full agreement." She pressed her lips tight and nodded, as though reassuring herself. "It was the right thing to do."

"I'd like to ask you some questions about Logan?" Ryan said.

"Of course, though I don't know what I'll be able to tell you. I mean, we met, but it wasn't as though we'd grown close or anything."

"Did you stay in touch with Logan?"

She folded her hands on the table. "Yes, we exchanged a couple of messages."

"Text messages or via social media?"

"Oh." She smiled brightly. "I'm not on social media. Neither are the children. I don't think it's good for the soul."

They clearly weren't going to get anything they might be able to link to the kind of messages Logan had been receiving. Ryan couldn't help thinking she probably had the better deal on that.

"When was the last time you heard from Logan?" he asked.

"Not long after the show aired. I think he wanted to know how I felt about it all."

"How did he seem?"

"Fine. Just like he had when we first met. I didn't get the impression he was worried about anything, if that's what you mean." She frowned. "You don't think Logan's death had anything to do with the television show, do you? I couldn't stand it if I thought I might have somehow been a catalyst for that awful thing to have happened to him?"

"It is an avenue we're exploring, Mrs McIver."

She blinked, her eyes bright. "Oh, my goodness. I was hoping you'd say no."

"That's why we need you to tell us everything you know, even if it seems like something small and insignificant."

"Gosh, I don't know what to say." She twisted her hands together in her lap. "My mind has gone blank. I'm sure Logan's family knew far more about him than I possibly could."

"We have spoken with them as well."

She shook her head. "That poor family. Losing a son that way, and after everything that poor boy had already been through. Have you ever lost someone you love, Detective?"

"No," he lied. "I haven't."

He sensed Mallory's questioning stare, but the truth was that he couldn't stand for the vicar's wife to start telling him things like 'God must have wanted Hayley back' or that she was in a better place. There had been no better place for Hayley than with her parents who had loved her. He needed to remain professional, and he didn't want to get into an argument about how he didn't believe there could be a God in world where such terrible things happened to innocent people.

She gave him a sympathetic smile, as though he'd missed out on something. "You're lucky to have never gone through that pain."

Mallory gave a light cough. "Sorry to interrupt, boss, but we have to be back in the office for the briefing."

"Yes, of course."

He was grateful to her for giving him an excuse to get out of the situation. It seemed Clare McIver was a dead end as far as leads went.

They both rose to their feet.

"Thank you for your time, Mrs McIver," he thanked her. "And I truly am sorry for your loss."

They left the house, holding jackets over their heads and moving at a jog to avoid the bad weather. Rain pelted down on them as they ran for the car. Ryan waited until they were safely within the interior before he spoke.

"Well, that was full-on."

She agreed. "Yes, I couldn't live like that. Always thinking about God before everything else. I wonder what the kids made of it all. This religious parent going on television and talking about their dad. They're at that age where they start to make up their own minds about things, maybe even rebel a little. It must be hard having this almost evangelical dead parent they need to live up to now."

"I know this sounds bad," Ryan said, "but she almost seems to thrive on the attention."

"I felt that, too. Like she enjoys having someone she can put on a pedestal, while everyone else feels sorry for her."

"Some people do thrive on that kind of thing. You get those parents who deliberately make their kids sick because they want the attention from the doctors. Not that I'm saying this is the same situation. I mean, her husband's car accident was already investigated, and it surely isn't enough of a motive to want Logan Foss dead."

"Plus, we're looking for a strong man," Mallory said, "and she definitely isn't that."

"That doesn't mean she couldn't have had an accomplice, though. And yes, the car accident was investigated, but maybe there was more to it and the investigating officers just didn't see it because they didn't have this additional information." He thought for a moment. "It might be a long shot, but I think we should go to the hospital where Gregory was taken that night, see if we can track down some of the staff who were working then, see if they remember what kind of frame of mind Clare McIver was in when she turned off her husband's life support. They might remember something."

"Good idea.

Ryan started the engine.

# Chapter Twenty-Two

They went to the intensive care unit, where Gregory McIver had spent his final hours before the machines that were keeping him alive were switched off and his body was harvested for the organs that would go on to save several lives.

Ryan headed straight to reception and showed his ID to the young male nurse sitting behind the desk. "You had a patient here three months ago. Gregory McIver. We need to speak to whoever was working on the ward on the day he was brought in."

He frowned. "That was some time ago. I'd need to check the old schedule."

"That's fine. We can wait."

"Okay, just give me a moment."

Ryan and Mallory stepped back from the desk to give the nurse some space and allow anyone else who might need access some room, too. The ward was busy, with staff rushing around and families of patients looking worried.

"Must be awful," Mallory said, "having someone lying in one of those beds."

"Yes, it is." Ryan had been here before. Was Cole Fielding still on this unit? He wasn't sure.

She shot him a glance. "Sorry.

The nurse behind the desk stood and beckoned them back over. "Okay, I found out who was on then. Fiona Gill and

Tamari Harvey were the two nurses. His doctor was Mr Allen, one of our consultants."

"Are any of those people on today? We could do with talking to them?"

"Oh, Tamari is on. Let me buzz her."

A young black woman appeared, her braided hair caught back in a knot at her nape. Her gaze flicked between the two of them. "How can I help?"

"Is there somewhere we can speak?" Ryan asked. He flipped open his ID for her to see. "It's about a patient you had here three months ago."

"Sure. Come through to the quiet room. I think it's free."

He and Mallory followed her to a room that contained a sofa and a couple of chairs. In the middle was a table that held a box of tissues and a jug of water with a stack of plastic cups next to it. In the corner was a toy box, used to distract small children when serious conversations needed to be had with the adults.

They each took a seat, and Mallory pulled out a notebook to jot everything down.

"What can I do for you, Detectives?" Tamari said.

Ryan jumped straight in. "You were working here the day a vicar called Gregory McIver was brought in after a car accident. He was brain dead, and his family agreed to donate his organs. This was three months ago. I don't suppose it rings any bells?"

She nodded. "Yes, I remember. That was hard to forget. We had to get security involved."

This surprised Ryan. "You did? Why?"

"There was a big commotion here, right before he was taken off the ventilator."

"What kind of commotion?"

"A man showed up. I'm not sure if he was related to them in some way, but he wanted to get into the room, even when the hospital staff tried to stop him. We had to call security. It was clear he didn't agree with the decisions the wife was making."

"The decisions? You mean to turn off life support and donate his organs?"

"Yes. This man found the whole thing extremely distressing and seemed to think he had some say in what was going on."

Ryan frowned. "And you're sure it's the same person? Gregory McIver?"

"Of course. The fact he was a vicar made him memorable."

"Do you have any idea who the man was? Another family member, perhaps?" If it was a brother or cousin, he didn't understand why Clare wouldn't have mentioned that to them.

"No, sorry, I don't."

"It was the wife's decision, though, wasn't it?" Ryan checked. "I mean, at the end of the day, the organ donation is the wife's choice?"

She sat back and crossed her legs. "Ultimately, yes, it's the choice of the spouse. We have an opt-out system now, where unless you expressly opt out of being an organ donor, it'll be taken that you did want to be one, but obviously if the next of kin is desperately against it, we wouldn't force them to sign their loved one's bodies over for organ donation."

"And Gregory McIver hadn't opted out?"

"No, he hadn't, and the family were happy to continue with the donation, so we had no reason to believe it wasn't what he would have wanted."

Ryan thought for a moment. "Did his wife know who the man was?"

She shrugged. "They didn't come face to face or anything. She stayed in the room with the kids, and the blinds were drawn for privacy. He kept saying that he had more right to be in there than she did, that Gregory would have wanted him there."

"He definitely knew Gregory then?"

"Oh, yes. He was crying and trying to fight off our security staff. We had to threaten to call the police. It was all really awful to watch. Emotions were clearly running high."

"But no one thought to get this man's name."

"The security staff might have."

Ryan turned to Mallory. "Can you check that out?"

She nodded. "Absolutely."

"What about the CCTV?" he asked Tamari. "Is it possible the man was caught on camera?"

The nurse looked a little helpless. "Again, that's security who deal with things like that. It doesn't have anything to do with us, but I'll be surprised if the hospital keeps the footage for this long. Cloud storage can get expensive, especially when a place has a lot of cameras. Plus, the hospital is all about saving money these days."

Ryan understood. "Can you give me a description of the man at all?"

She bit her lower lip. "Oh, gosh. It was some time ago."

"Anything you can remember would be helpful. What race was he? Did he have any tattoos or scars? How did he wear his hair?"

"He was white and in his forties, I think. Tall. I remember thinking that it was going to be harder for security to throw him out because he wasn't exactly a small man. He was quite smartly dressed. I remember noticing because he ended up ruffled from his struggles with security, and it really didn't suit him. I didn't notice any tattoos or anything, sorry."

"Hair colour?" Ryan prompted. "Eye colour."

"Light-brown hair, I think. I couldn't tell you what eye colour he had."

Ryan offered her a smile. "That's okay. You've been very helpful."

"Can I go now?" she asked. "I have patients to take care of."

"Yes, of course."

She smiled at them and went back her work.

Ryan turned to Mallory. "Well, *that* was interesting. Why wouldn't Clare have mentioned any of that to us?"

Mallory frowned. "Do you think this could be connected to Logan Foss's murder?"

"Honestly, I'm really not sure how all of this ties together right now. I think we need to speak to Clare again and see what she has to say about all of this. You have to admit it's a little strange."

"It would have been a highly emotive time. Maybe it was a friend of Gregory's."

"Is that the normal behaviour of a friend?" Ryan dragged his hand through his hair. "We're going to need to speak with the other members of staff who were on that day, see if they remember anything else, and go to security and see what CCTV footage they can pull up."

He hoped he wasn't going on a wild goose chase that had nothing to do with Logan Foss's murder. But in his experience, when people lied, it meant they were hiding something, and when people hid things, it normally meant they were up to no good.

# Chapter Twenty-Three

Ryan delegated the work to chase up the information from the hospital and got back into the office. He got himself another coffee from the machine. His hangover had faded into the background now, though his eyes were still gritty, and he desperately could have done with a nap.

He carried the coffee back to his desk and sat down.

His mobile phone rang, the name Townsend appearing on screen.

It was the sergeant who'd been in charge of Cole Fielding's case. His heart rate instantly picked up. What now? Was Cole talking? Had he spoken to Ryan's colleagues and told them exactly what had happened the night of Cole's 'accident'? Did Townsend want to talk to him to find out his side of the story?

All these things raced through his mind while he stared at the name on-screen. He needed to answer it, but his body didn't seem able to respond to his mind.

"Boss," one of his DC's called over. "Phone."

The words jolted Ryan out of his stupor, and he snatched up the mobile and swiped the screen to answer. His ears felt like they were full of bees, buzzing, the sergeant's voice distant.

"Ryan? Are you there?"

"Yes, sorry, I'm here. What's up?"

He heard Townsend take a deep breath before speaking.

"Cole Fielding died last night."

Ryan froze. "What? I thought he was improving?"

"He had been. I don't know the details yet, but it seemed his death was somewhat...unexpected. I mean, not that unexpected, considering how ill he's been for such a long time, but like you say, the doctors thought he was making an improvement."

A wave of dizziness swept over Ryan, and he found himself reaching for his desk to keep himself from sliding off his chair.

"Will there be an investigation into his death? I mean, will they do a post-mortem to find out why he died?"

"Yes, one is already being carried out. If the doctors don't know the cause behind him suddenly passing away, they're going to want answers, if only to prevent it happening to another patient."

"Of course." His mind raced. "Do-do you know exactly when he died?"

"No, I don't, but I believe it was sometime during the night."

Ryan cast his mind back over the previous evening. After the argument with Donna, he'd gone home and, against his better judgement, had opened the whiskey bottle. What could he recall? There was definitely a blank spot, or at least it was fuzzy around the edges. Could he have gone into the hospital?

No, he'd have remembered going out.

Even so, unease settled like a lead weight in his chest, and his heart beat so fast it felt like a flutter. The truth was, he didn't trust himself. Hadn't he gone to the hospital himself to see Cole after he'd heard about Cole waking up? He'd thought about it then, how easy it would have been to put a pillow over Cole's face and just end things. It had been a fleeting consideration—not something he'd ever actually do, though.

But yes, there had been times when he'd wanted nothing more than for Cole to be dead. It was what the young man had deserved after stealing Hayley from their lives. Cole had ruined three lives that day—Hayley's, Donna's, and Ryan's. Cole shouldn't have been allowed to get away with that, and the handful of years Cole had spent inside had felt like an insult to them.

He should be relieved. With Cole dead, the truth of what had happened the night Cole had fallen from the bridge would never come out. But a part of him had wanted to know the truth.

Had he been the one responsible for putting Cole in hospital? Or had that just been his intrusive thoughts talking?

He remembered Townsend still on the end of the line. Ryan cleared his throat. "Thanks for letting me know. I appreciate it."

"No problem," Townsend said. "I thought it was the least you deserve after what you and your family have been through."

They hung up, and Ryan put his head in his hand.

He became conscious of Mallory standing nearby.

"You all right, boss? You've gone white."

He lifted his head. "Yeah, yeah. I'm fine. Just got some news, that's all."

"Everyone okay?"

"Yes...I mean, no." He scrubbed his hand over his face. "Cole Fielding is dead."

Her mouth dropped. Mallory knew Ryan and his family well enough to understand exactly who Cole Fielding was and what it meant to them.

"Oh, shit. Is...is that a good thing?"

"I'm not sure how I feel about it right now."

She grimaced. "I'm not surprised. That's a lot to take on."

He sat back and blew out a breath. "I guess it feels right. More like justice than the pathetic amount of time he spent in prison."

Mallory nodded. "I can understand that."

"I have to tell Donna."

"How do you think she's going to react?"

He touched the smooth, glass face of his phone, as though teasing it to bring up Donna's number. "Honestly, I'm not sure. Maybe I'll wait a couple of days—just so she has had time to enjoy her all-clear diagnosis first."

"Why? Do you think she'd be upset?"

"Not at his death, but it will stir up a whole lot of emotions. No matter what Cole did, he's still a person, and it's hard to be pleased that another human being is dead. I mean, what does that say about us, that we can take pleasure from that kind of loss? Doesn't that make us just as bad as him?"

"You weren't the one who killed Cole. It's different."

*Wasn't he?* No, he wasn't. He had to keep reminding himself of that. No matter what his intrusive thoughts told him. He was never going to find out any differently now—the one person who might have said differently was finally dead—and no good would come from him torturing himself about it.

"I know that." He paused and bit his lower lip. "I went in to see him a few months ago."

Her eyebrows lifted. "Cole? Why?"

"To satisfy my curiosity, I guess. I heard he'd woken up, and I thought the next step would be him out of bed and walking around like nothing had happened. It wasn't like that, though. He was awake, but he didn't seem to know what was going on around him."

"Did he recognise you?"

Ryan remembered the fit Cole had experienced while he'd been there. Had that been because he'd known who Ryan was and he was scared of him? Or had Cole been clueless and it had simply been a coincidence?"

"Honestly, I'm not sure. I didn't stay for long, just long enough to see that Cole wasn't going to be walking out of there anytime soon."

"Did...did he say anything?"

"I don't think he was even capable of saying anything. One thing I knew for sure when I saw him that day was that the young man who'd run Hayley down didn't exist anymore. He was a shell of person."

She eyed him sympathetically. "I don't know what to say."

"You don't have to say anything. It's over now."

# Chapter Twenty-Four

Macie tugged at the front of her shirt anxiously and questioned her decision to come. The studio was huge, and she was sure she'd get lost. She prayed she wasn't going to have another panic attack.

Things had moved quickly the moment she'd replied to the Instagram message from the production team. Apparently, they were scheduled to record a new show, but things had needed to be rearranged due to the news that one of their previous guests had been murdered. Macie had been shocked to learn that it was the young man who'd previously been on the show meeting the donor family—the same people she was here to meet today.

The researcher told her that they would, of course, be talking about the tragic event, but that they didn't want to leave their audience on such a sombre topic. Having her there to show everyone that life did, indeed, go on, would be a huge help, both to the studio and to the donor family who were now suffering not one, but two losses.

How could she possibly have said no to that?

She entered the building and was immediately approached by security.

"Umm, I'm here for *Tova's Questions*," she told him.

"You need to sign in and get a security badge."

She followed him over to the desk and did as he'd requested, and he handed her a lanyard to loop over her neck.

"This way."

He jerked his thick neck to indicate for her to follow. She was relieved that he was going to take her where she needed to be rather than for her to try to navigate this airport hangar of a place.

He walked at a brisk pace, his long legs covering the ground swiftly, so she found herself half running to keep up. He pushed through double doors into a new set of corridors and spotted someone up ahead.

"Hey, I've got someone for your show, Tiffy," he called.

A girl in her twenties with pink hair and who was chewing gum, turned to face her.

He drew to a halt. "I'll leave you in her capable hands."

Macie threw him a smile of thanks.

The girl came bounding over. "Hi. I'm Tiffany, one of the runners here. I need to get you down to makeup."

"Makeup?"

"Yeah, trust me. You don't want to go on camera looking like that. The studio lights will completely wash you out."

She thought she'd put a decent amount of effort into her appearance before leaving the house, but she guessed she needed to leave it up to the professionals. "Oh, right. We're filming already, are we?"

"Yes, did no one tell you? It's a special production due to the tragic loss of Logan Foss, so we're going to be broadcasting live tonight."

Her eyes widened. "A live broadcast? I didn't know that."

"It'll be fine, honest. Come on, this way."

Shell-shocked, Macie followed the girl. Surely they were going to have some rehearsals or something? They wouldn't just throw her onstage and broadcast it to thousands of people?

She could feel herself getting panicky again and took some deliberate deep breaths.

"Sorry, but is anyone going to run me through what I'm supposed to be doing? I've never been on television before. I'm a little out of my depth here."

*I'm completely out of my depth. I'm so out of my depth I'm drowning.*

"Oh, of course. Tova and Emmett, the director, will meet with you first and run through everything. Leave everything in their hands. Tova is a total professional. All you have to do is follow her lead and she'll make sure you come off beautifully on-screen."

"Really?"

"Yes, you've seen her show, haven't you? Has she ever made one of her guests look bad?"

Macie released a breath. Tiffany had a point.

She was ushered into a tiny room filled with mirrors. A makeup artist sat her in a chair and put more makeup on her than she had ever worn in her life. It looked completely unnatural to her, but she was assured it was normal and would be perfect on-screen.

She wondered if the donor family was here yet. Would she pass them in the corridors or backstage? Would they recognise her? Did they even know her name?

"There, all done," the makeup artist declared. "Let's get you through to the green room."

Macie found herself being hurried down the corridor once more and into a separate room where refreshments had been laid out. "Help yourself to anything you want."

Macie thanked her.

She glanced over to find she wasn't alone. A well-dressed man in his forties stared at her, his handsome face unreadable. Was she in the wrong place? She offered him a nervous smile, and instantly the expression vanished and was replaced by a wide one of his own.

"Let me guess," he said as he strode towards her. "You're Macie Ostrow."

"Yes, I am." She shook the hand he offered her. His grip was a little too firm—almost painfully so.

"I'm the show's director, Emmett Callan. Thank you for saving our bacon by deciding to do this show. It would have been a depressing one otherwise."

He pulled a face as though to make her laugh, but she wasn't sure anything about this was particularly funny. They were all here because people had died.

"It seemed like the right thing to do," she said.

"Of course. Have you met Tova yet? No? You must come and meet her. She's my right-hand woman, and this show literally wouldn't be anything without her. I keep trying to tell her what a help she is with all of this," he gestured aimlessly around the big space, "but I don't think she ever hears me."

Emmett had a kind of nervous energy that came from either too much coffee or perhaps some kind of anxiety disorder. He seemed to be overcompensating for something with a loud voice and big gestures. He was the kind of person she immediately felt smaller around.

"I'm a bit nervous," she admitted. "I didn't realise this was going to be live."

His eyebrows shot up. "You didn't know the show was filmed before a live audience?"

"Well, yes, but Tiffany told me this one was going out live?"

He flapped a hand. "It's basically the same thing. In fact, this will be easier because there isn't an audience involved. It'll be just like you're having a chat with Tova and then coming face to face with some people who can't wait to meet you."

The way he put it did make it sound pretty easy.

"Oh, okay."

"Let's go and find Tova," he said, already heading to the door. "She'll put you right at ease."

With little choice, she followed him back out of the green room and down the corridor to where he stopped outside a door with a star on the front and Tova Lane's name written inside it.

He knocked on the door. "You decent in there? I have someone who wants to meet you."

A high voice called back, "Come on in."

The director opened the door just as a blonde woman spun around in a chair to face them.

Macie recognised Tova Lane from the television. The other woman was tinier than she'd expected, barely over five feet, and there didn't seem to be an ounce of body fat on her. At a glance, she would have thought Tova to be in her late twenties to early thirties, but up close, it was clear she was at least a decade older, the fine lines across her brow and spanning from her eyes and lips that would have been disguised by makeup on-screen.

It was hard not to feel at least a little starstruck in her presence. She seemed so well put together and confident. The complete opposite of how Macie felt.

Tova got to her feet and greeted her warmly, clutching both hands between hers and shaking them.

"Thank you so much for coming. I can't tell you how much this will mean to both me and my viewers that we're getting a continuation of this story. It's like bringing a family back together again."

Was it? She wasn't so sure about that. These people were strangers. She definitely didn't feel like she was about to meet family—she felt like she was about to meet someone who'd suffered the worst loss imaginable, and she'd benefited from it.

"Will I get to meet them before the filming?" she asked.

"No. It's far more impactful if we can do the first meeting on camera. Otherwise, it all feels a bit watered down, you know?"

"I guess so."

A fresh wave of nerves swept through her. What was she doing here? What did she think she was going to achieve? Had she wanted to know more about the person whose heart was now beating in her chest? Like she could understand a little more about who she was supposed to be now.

Could she leave? Say she'd changed her mind? But the embarrassment of running overwhelmed her fear of doing the interview. They'd have to explain to the public why they no longer had a show, and she would be the cause of that.

"There's no need to be nervous," Tova said, as though picking up on her thoughts. "We're going to do a dress rehearsal of all the questions I'll ask you when we're live. I promise I won't ask you anything you're not already prepared for, okay?"

"Okay."

The next couple of hours went by in a whirlwind of activity. Just as she'd promised, Tova took her through everything that was going to be said, and she was given directions about which way she needed to walk onto the stage, and where she should sit, and what angle she should face. They went over it again and again, until Macie finally felt like she was getting the hang of things. To her surprise, she actually started to relax and enjoy herself. Everyone was fussing over her, the makeup artist darting in every now and then to dust her nose with more powder.

Finally, the time arrived to begin the real thing.

Macie's nerves kicked in afresh, but she'd lost any urge to make a run for it. Everyone had been so encouraging, she'd finally convinced herself that she was doing the right thing.

She sat backstage while Tova began the show. The first segment was going to be about the tragic murder of Logan Foss, then they would bring the donor's family—who were waiting on the other side of the set, deliberately kept separate from her—and they would talk about what Logan had meant to them and how they were feeling now.

Macie had Tiffany, one of the runners, with her while all that went on. Tiffany kept smiling at her and whispering words of encouragement. Macie knotted her hands in front of her and shifted from foot to foot. Her nerves were almost overwhelming now, but she couldn't do anything about it.

"Go!" Tiffany hissed at her. "It's time.

She gave Macie a little nudge in the back, and Macie staggered forward. For one horrifying second, she thought she was going to make her entrance by falling on the stage, but she managed to right herself and kept going. She plastered a wide smile onto her face and stepped into the bright lights.

Onstage, a woman in her late forties, with dark curly hair that was white at the temples, stood with two children, a boy and a girl. The kids were lanky teens or pre-teens and were the same height as their mother. They all wore identical smiles, but there was something about the expressions that didn't feel quite real. Macie thought that there was a good chance the smile on her own face was exactly the same.

"Macie," Tova said, "meet Clare McIver and her children, Martha and Simon."

The woman, Clare, opened her arms to Macie, and automatically Macie walked into them.

Clare hugged her tight, and Macie was hugely conscious of the place where her heart pressed against the other woman's chest.

"Oh my gosh, how pretty you are," Clare gushed, swiping at a tear.

"Oh, thank you."

Clare introduced her children. "This is Simon, he's fourteen, and Martha, who is twelve."

Macie had never been great around kids, but she nodded at them. "I'm so sorry about your dad."

The boy gave that same tight smile and glanced at the floor. "Thanks."

They all took seats, side by side, on the stools that had been set out for them. Macie sat between Tova and Clare, just as she'd been directed to earlier.

"Clare, why don't you tell Macie a little bit about your husband, Gregory."

"He was a wonderful man," Clare began. "He was a vicar."

A shock like a tremor passed through Macie. A vicar? How could she have the heart of a vicar? Again, that feeling of not being good enough swept through her, and she instantly wished she hadn't agreed to this. That was too much to live up to.

Unaware of Macie's reaction, Clare continued.

"He would have loved to know his heart went to such a vibrant young woman. To see you go on and live your life because of him would have made him so happy. He adored his family and the church. Everything he did was for other people." She lifted both hands. "I'm not saying he didn't ever think about himself—he was human and had his little slipups just like the rest of us—but he always got himself back on the right path again."

She spoke about him as though he were an angel, as though desperate to make everyone understand how good her dead husband had been, not only when he'd been alive, but also continuing into his death.

The boy was staring at his mother. Suddenly, he jumped off the stool and rounded on her. "Stop it! Just stop it already."

Her mouth dropped open in shock. "Simon? What are you doing?"

"I can't stand it anymore. Hearing you go on and on about Dad."

A muscle twitched beside her eye. "Darling, don't speak to me like that."

"Stop lying then!"

A sense of shock and awkwardness descended over them all. What was it she was lying about?

Clare had gone pale. Her eyes shone with unshed tears, and the smile stretched across her face looked painful.

Tova stepped in. "Time for an ad break, folks. Let's pick this back up after we've heard from our sponsors."

# Chapter Twenty-Five

Tova ran out into the rain. It was torrential now, and she wished she'd thought to bring her umbrella.

She'd finally made herself leave the studio. It was late, but she'd stayed to monitor the fallout on social media, or at least that's what she told herself. She wouldn't have admitted that she was also a little scared of going back to her flat alone in case there might be another card or something waiting for her.

Doing that live show had been a big mistake.

Perhaps they'd been pushing things by bringing the children back on the show. After all, it hadn't been long at all since they'd lost their father, and no one had ever consulted them about what they'd wanted to do with their father's organs. It must be much harder for them to understand, even though they weren't small children, and then their mother dragged them onto a television show to talk about it.

As she drove, Tova experienced a twinge of guilt. Hadn't she helped to exploit the same children in order to create a good story? The old heartstrings were always twanged more firmly when children were involved, and their mother had assured Tova's production team that the kids were as excited about meeting their father's donor recipients as much as she was. That it would give them comfort to see how life had gone on, even after their dad's death.

She approached a junction and braked and hit the clutch to change gear. From out of nowhere, the power died from the engine.

"No!" The car slowed to a halt. She hit the 'push' button in the hope to restart it, but nothing happened. "Shit. Shit, shit, shit."

She should have hung on to the hire car.

Tova twisted in her seat to get an idea of where she was. It was late, so the roads were quiet, and the rain made it impossible to see much. Now her windscreen wipers weren't even working, and the glass was like she was sitting under a waterfall.

She reached for her bag and fished her phone out. At least she had breakdown cover. She dialled the emergency number, and when the person on the other end answered, she explained where she was and what had happened.

"I don't have anyone in your area right now," he told her. "It's going to be at least an hour before anyone can reach you."

"Seriously?"

"It is almost midnight."

She threw up a hand in exasperation, even though the man on the end of the line couldn't see her. "Exactly. It's not as though it's rush hour and everyone is out on the road. You should have more people available, not less."

"There are less people on call in the middle of the night, due to the fact that the vast majority of people are in bed."

She picked up on his curt tone and bristled. "So, you're saying it's my fault I've broken down and the service I've paid for is crap because I should be in bed right now? I supposed it won't make the blindest bit of difference that I've been working and I'm absolutely shattered?"

He sounded irritated. "Like I said, the nearest call-out is still an hour away."

"And I'm just supposed to sit in my car, alone, at midnight, for an hour until they get here?"

"Do you have anyone else you could call to come and sit with you?"

"No! That's the whole point of paying you."

Annoyed, she ended the call and tossed her phone onto the passenger seat.

What was she supposed to do? The place where the car was, on the corner of the junction, meant she couldn't just abandon it. She glanced over her shoulder. Should she even remain sitting in the car? What if someone came racing around the corner and didn't see her and slammed into the back or side? She was sure she'd read that it was dangerous to stay in a broken-down car, but was that just on a motorway? Even if it was unsafe, the thought of getting out and standing on the side of the road at this time of night was even less appealing. The rain had grown heavier the longer she'd sat here, and she didn't want to stand out in it and get wet. Her hazard lights flashed, illuminating the rain and the road around her.

Maybe someone would stop and offer her some assistance.

She didn't like how vulnerable she felt. Even if someone did stop, if it was a man on his own, she'd only get her hackles up, no matter how nice they seemed. She didn't trust anyone these days.

Tova picked her phone back up, wondering if she should post something online—partly to complain about the supposed roadside assistance company that was leaving her stranded at this time of night, but also so there would be a record of her final position, should something happen to her. But she stopped herself. That wouldn't be a smart move either. She'd be announcing to the world that she was alone and vulnerable.

Loneliness swept over her, stealing her breath. How was it possible to have reached her age, and have her position in life, and yet not have a single person who she could call up at midnight and ask for help? She had people in her life, but no one with that kind of intimacy that she didn't feel as though she was intruding or making her problem their problem.

She tapped her nails against the cover of her phone and glanced around again. A swathe of yellow cut through the dark and rain as a car approached. Even though she knew it wouldn't be the assistance service, a part of her still hoped that the man on the phone had got it wrong.

But the car drove past, and she exhaled a breath.

She went back to her phone and pulled up her social media. Her stomach twisted. There were a lot of messages and comments from people complaining about the exploitation of the children on the show.

Headlights lit up her rear-view mirror, and she twisted to see if there was any chance the assistance had arrived.

A vehicle pulled in a short distance behind her.

Tova froze. It wasn't the assistance van, she knew that much. The rain had grown even heavier now, pelting against the windows, blurring her view. She could tell it was some kind of saloon car, in a dark colour, but that was all.

What was the driver doing? Had they stopped to see if she needed help? And if so, why hadn't they got out of the car yet? Perhaps they were waiting for the rain to abate.

Or maybe it had nothing to do with her whatsoever and they'd just pulled over because their phone had rung or something. But it seemed like a fairly modern vehicle, so wouldn't they have hands-free set up in it? They might have stopped for a different reason. Their car might have broken down as well, and it was just a coincidence that they'd stopped not far behind her.

Tova remained twisted around in her seat, staring out the back window. The headlights of the car were still on, which also impeded her view. Did the driver realise the lights were half blinding her? Maybe they'd done it on purpose.

Were they waiting for her to get out of the car? Should she? If she got out of her own car and walked towards theirs, perhaps with her phone in her hand, videoing what she was seeing, then she'd at least get the number plate on record and see if she recognised either the vehicle or the person behind the wheel.

Maybe she should be proactive and approach them herself instead of hiding out in here? No, that was a bad idea. She was at least safe in here.

Quickly, she locked all the doors. No one could get in.

Unless they smashed the windows...

Her imagination was getting the better of her. She wasn't trapped in some teen horror movie. She was in the middle of Bristol.

Another car drove past, and this one kept going.

Shit. The driver was still sitting there.

Her heart pounded, and she tightened her hands into fists. What the fuck was going on?

Fuck it, she'd call an Uber and just abandon her car. She didn't care if she got a ticket or even if the car was towed. She just wanted to get out of there. She checked the app. The nearest Uber was still seventeen minutes away.

Jesus. What the fuck was wrong with everyone tonight? No one wanted to work anymore, it seemed.

It was now approaching twelve-thirty, and the weather was miserable. That was why no one was out tonight. It wasn't their fault she'd got herself into a situation.

She glanced back at the car. It was still there and, as far as she could tell, the driver was still behind the wheel.

Maybe she should call the police. After all, she was a traffic hazard here, wasn't she? She wouldn't just be calling because it was late and she was alone, and after all the creepy things that had been happening lately, she was on edge.

She remembered the card the detective had given her. Did she still have it? She rifled through her handbag. Yes, she did. DI Chase of the Major Crimes Investigation Team of the Avon and Somerset Police. He was a police officer, so he'd be used to getting calls about things at crazy times of the day and night. She didn't think it was a job you just checked in and out of.

Desperate, she plugged the mobile number into her phone and placed it to her ear. *Please answer.*

"DI Chase." His voice was groggy. "Who's this?"

She'd clearly woken him, and her stomach twisted with remorse. "Umm, Detective, hi. I'm sorry to call you at this ungodly hour. My name is Tova Lane. I don't know if you remember me?"

She heard the rustle of bedsheets as he must have sat up in bed.

"Tova Lane. Yes, of course, I remember. What's going on? Do you know what time it is?"

She didn't answer that question. "You remember someone graffitied my car and I got that weird card? Well, now I've broken down, and someone has pulled in behind me, and they're not doing anything. They're just sitting there, and it's freaking me out."

"Have you called a recovery service?"

She clutched her phone tighter. "Yes, but they can't get here for a whole hour. I'm feeling vulnerable. What if it's the same person as the one who did the damage to my car and sent me that card?" She spoke her darkest fear. "What if it's the same person who murdered Logan Foss?"

His voice was deep and calm and soothing. "Have you locked your car doors?"

"Yes, I have."

"And the other person hasn't done anything yet?"

She checked back over her shoulder. "No, they're just sitting there. It's been about fifteen minutes now."

"It might not have anything to do with you."

"Maybe not, but with everything that's happened, you can't blame me for freaking out."

He sighed. "Okay, Tova. Tell me where you are."

"I'll send you a pin on Google Maps."

She did as she'd said so he knew her exact location.

"Got it. I'm on my way, but I'm going to get a squad car to come drive by, make sure whoever is behind you knows that we're around, okay?"

"Thank you, Detective. I can't tell you how relieved I am to know you're there for me."

# Chapter Twenty-Six

Ryan drove through the rain, the windscreen wipers slashing back and forth, trying to keep up with the deluge. What the hell was he thinking, coming out in this? He'd already got a couple of uniformed officers on their way to the scene. It wasn't as though he needed to be there. Yet he'd still chosen to get out of his perfectly warm, comfortable bed in the middle of the night and come out in the pissing rain.

He wasn't so self-unaware as to realise that it had something to do with the fact the person who had called him happened to be female, blonde, pretty, and somewhat famous. If it had been a fifty-year-old bloke who'd made the call, he might have found himself giving a slightly different response.

With little traffic on the road, it didn't take him long to reach the spot where Tova had said she'd broken down. Sure enough, a patrol car was parked up behind her vehicle, and the driver's door of her car was open. He spotted her sitting inside, staying dry, while she spoke to the two police officers.

He didn't see any sign of the car she'd reported.

She looked like she'd been crying.

"DI Chase. I'm so sorry for getting you out of bed."

"That's okay." He turned to the uniformed officer. "Any sign of the vehicle?"

"No. Ms Lane says it drove off just before we got here."

"It was like whoever was driving knew you were coming," she said in a rush. "It really worried me, though. It was so creepy, them just sitting there, not doing anything."

"Did you get a look at the driver at all?" Ryan asked.

"No. He kept his headlights on, and with the dark and the rain, it was impossible to see anything."

"So, it might not have even been a man driving."

She hesitated. "Well, no, I guess not. But how many women would just stop on the side of the road at this time of night for no good reason?"

"You did," he pointed out.

"I broke down. I didn't have much choice."

"Perhaps the other person was having car trouble, too."

It was a valid point, but he could see Tova wasn't buying it. She was visibly shaken, her cheeks devoid of colour and her hands trembling when she lifted one to push her hair back from her face. It was understandable. Someone she'd been involved with on a professional level had been murdered and she felt she was being targeted. Whether that was by the same person, however, it was impossible to say.

"We've got Automatic Number Plate Recognition cameras around this area," Ryan told her. "Considering the background to all of this, I'll go through the footage and see if they've captured any vehicles around that time that might match up to your one."

Her expression brightened. "Really? You'd do that?"

"Of course. If we can come up with a number plate, I'll go and have a chat with the owner, see if we can get all this cleared up."

He hoped he'd be able to tell her the person had perhaps been hit by a sudden bout of nausea and had needed to pull over, and it was simply a coincidence that it happened to be the same place Tova had been stopped. If the whole thing was completely innocent, it might put Tova's mind at rest.

"What about getting fingerprints from the card I gave you?" she asked.

"I haven't had any results back yet, but I'll chase them up in the morning."

Behind, them, a recovery van parked up.

"About bloody time," Tova muttered.

"Not impressed with the service?" Ryan said, amused.

"Yours was far better."

The rain had eased off a fraction.

"Excuse me a minute," she said and ran over to the van. "I called your lot over an hour ago."

The driver looked bemused. "What are the police all doing here?"

"Car is a hazard where it's stopped. They didn't want there to be any accidents."

The lie seemed to trip smoothly off her tongue. She clearly didn't want to explain herself to the bloke, which was understandable.

"Okay, let's see if I can get you back on the road again."

"You need a lift anywhere?" Ryan offered. He needed to get back, hopefully to get some more kip, but most likely just to dry off and get ready for another day at the office.

"No, I'm fine now I'm not on my own, but thank you. I'm sorry I made you come all the way down here."

"No problem, Ms Lane. It was good to see you again. Stay safe."

# Chapter Twenty-Seven

As he'd predicted, Ryan hadn't managed to get any more sleep.

Instead, he went into the office early. He'd go through the ANPR camera footage and see if he could spot anything suspicious about the person who'd followed Tova Lane last night. It wasn't likely the car had anything to do with the Logan Foss case, but any lead was a good lead at this point. They were still no closer to finding out who had murdered him or why.

One by one, his team trickled into the office to join him. The atmosphere wasn't great. The initial rush of a murder case had worn off, and now everyone was stuck behind their desks watching CCTV footage and chasing down the owners of vehicles caught in the area at the time Logan Foss had been taken from his flat to the warehouse. But it had been rush-hour traffic in Bristol, and over the space of a couple of hours, that meant checking up on a lot of different cars and vans. It was boring, monotonous work, but it had to be done.

Dev Kharral approached his desk.

"Boss, I don't know if this is of any use or not, but I was going back over what Cameron James—the teenager who found the body—had said about seeing a car two weeks prior to the murder. There was a mobile speed camera on the Bath Road that night. I haven't narrowed it down by much, mind you, but I thought we could cross-reference the vehicles to any that we might have caught the evening Logan Foss was taken."

"That's excellent work, thanks. Let's keep our fingers crossed. We could do with a solid lead on this now."

The longer things dragged on, the less likely it was that they would make an arrest.

Dev left and was quickly replaced by Mallory.

"I don't suppose you caught the interview on *Tova's Questions* last night?" she asked.

"*Tova's Questions*?"

He hadn't told her that he'd gone out in the middle of the night to 'rescue' the host of the show. "No, I didn't."

"They interviewed one of the other recipients of the organs that Gregory McIver donated, a woman called Macie Ostrow. She met with Clare and the children onstage. Only it didn't quite go as planned. One of the donor's children lost it and started accusing Clare of lying."

Ryan frowned. "They broadcast that?"

"Yep. It was all done live."

Was that part of the reason Tova had been so flustered last night? Had her show gone badly, and she'd freaked out over nothing?

"That's strange. What was she supposed to have been lying about?"

"I'm not sure, but anyone who is connected to someone who's been murdered and is then accused of lying makes red flags flash up for me. That, combined with what we were told at the hospital, makes me feel like she wasn't being completely honest with us."

Ryan nodded. "You're right. I think we should have a talk to Clare McIver again."

"OH, YOU'RE BACK."

Clare didn't seem very pleased to see them when she opened the door to find the two detectives standing on her doorstep once more.

Ryan stepped forward. "I'm afraid we've had some new developments and we needed to ask you some more questions, just to get things smoothed out."

"I guess you'd better come in then."

She retreated into the hallway to let them into the house. Once more, Ryan found himself seated around the kitchen table, being stared at by all the religious artefacts and paintings on the wall.

"I know this must be difficult for you," he began, "but could you tell me about those few hours after you were told your husband was brain dead, and you then went on to decide to donate his organs and turn off the machines."

Her eyes narrowed. "You're right, that is very difficult—the hardest moment of my life, if you must know. What could this possibly have to do with Logan Foss's murder?"

"If you could just answer the question, please."

"You want to know what happened? We cried and we said goodbye and we cried some more. And then finally the machines were turned off—so many machines. Do you know what the hardest thing of all was, Detectives? It's one thing no one warns you about when someone is a heart-beating donor. It all has to happen very quickly in order for the organ to still be viable, so it looked like Greg was still alive, and we just left him there."

It was a heartbreaking story, but Ryan couldn't allow himself to be distracted. "So, nothing unusual happened?"

Tears welled in her eyes. "I'd say my husband and father of my children dying was pretty unusual."

"But nothing outside of that?"

She wrung her hands, her lips thinning "What are you getting at, Detective?"

"We spoke to someone who was working that day, and they report there being a disturbance. A man showed up and caused a scene, shouting that it wasn't your place to choose to turn off the machines and donate his organs."

"I don't know what you're talking about."

"Mrs McIver, I have several witnesses who state there was a man who came to the hospital the day your husband died and wanted to get into the room. We have CCTV footage of the incident. Are you telling me you don't know who that was?" It was a slight fib. They didn't actually have any CCTV footage just yet, but that didn't mean it didn't exist.

She glanced down at her hands. "Oh, yes. That."

"You remember now?" he prompted.

She still wasn't meeting his eye. "I don't know who he was. I was out of my mind with grief and, all of a sudden, this lunatic is trying to get into his room and is screaming obscenities. He terrified my children, and the hospital staff had to get security to remove him."

"You didn't recognise him at all?"

"No, I didn't get a look at him. My attention was on my children and husband, and I was devastated by grief. That whole period is just a blur. All I remember was a whole lot of shouting and crying, and a lot of movement out in the corridor that I couldn't see through the blinds."

Ryan leaned forward slightly. "Do you think he might have been a friend of your husband's?"

"How should I know?" she snapped. "He could have been a complete stranger with mental health issues who thought he would come and mess with an already traumatised family."

Ryan checked his notes. "The nurse we spoke to believes the man knew your husband. He even used his name."

"He could have found out his name from anywhere. That doesn't mean anything."

It was clear this conversation was making her uncomfortable. Was it just that she found it difficult thinking back to what must have been the hardest moment of her life, or was there more to it? Did she know who this person was but was hiding the truth for some reason?

"What about your children?" Ryan prompted. "Would they have got a look at him?"

"No! Of course not."

Mallory stepped in. "Why did your son accuse you of lying on television last night?"

Clare stiffened. "I don't know."

Mallory raised her eyebrows. "Really? You have no idea what he was talking about?"

"No, I don't."

Ryan exhaled a breath of frustration. "Please, Mrs McIver. I can't help but feel as though you're holding something back from us. A man has been murdered, and he had a connection to you and your late husband, and now we're getting reports of disturbances the day the machines were switched off, and yet you don't seem to know what it was all about." Still, she didn't reply. Ryan tried a different tactic. "Where were you on the night of Logan Foss's murder?"

She straightened. "I was here, at home."

"Alone?"

"No, far from alone. I had a women's group prayer practise here. I had at least..." She thought for a moment. "At least six other people here, not including my children."

"And they were here from what time?"

"They arrived around six and then left by eleven."

"And your children?"

"They were here, too. Upstairs in their rooms. They would have been reading the Bible or doing homework."

"Are your children home now, Mrs McIver?"

"Yes, they're in their rooms. I gave them the day off. I thought after everything they've been through, they deserved it."

"Can you call them down, please? I'd like to ask them that for myself."

"They've been through enough, Detective, without being interrogated by the likes of you."

Ryan let his body language relax, his shoulders drop, and sat back. "It's a simple question. I promise I'll go easy on them, and you can be here, too."

He wondered why someone who was apparently so protective of her children would have dragged them onto a television show to be gawked at by hundreds of thousands of viewers. Was she trying to control the narrative? And if so, what was she hiding?

"Fine."

She called the children downstairs. They both seemed anxious, and Ryan offered them a smile. Their mother was right in that they had been through enough, and he wished he could get away with not questioning them, but the fact was, he felt as though their mother was lying. A man had been brutally murdered, and it was Ryan's job to find out who was responsible.

"Don't worry," Mallory reassured them. "You're not in any trouble. We just need to ask you some questions."

The children looked to each other for reassurance.

Ryan smiled. "It won't take long. You're Martha, right?" he said to the girl. "And you're Simon?"

They both nodded.

"You must miss your dad very much."

Again, they exchanged that same look. The kids knew something, Ryan was sure of it.

"I know this is hard to think about, but do you remember someone coming to the hospital the night your dad died?"

Clare let out a sigh. "It's okay, you can tell them."

"Yes," Simon said. "I remember."

"Do you know what his name was?"

The boy chewed at his lower lip. "I don't know his name or what he looks like, but I think he was Dad's friend. Dad didn't live at home before he died."

Ryan frowned. This was news. "He didn't? Where did he live?"

"He'd moved in with his friend."

Ryan refocused his attention on Clare. "Don't you think this is information you should have shared with us sooner?"

She bristled. "Why? We're not the ones on trial here. We haven't done anything wrong—quite the opposite. All I ever wanted to do was protect his reputation, to make sure everyone knew he was a good man and whatever...mistakes...he made towards the end wasn't really him. This man was sent to him by the Devil to tempt him, and I know he would have found his way back to me and back to God, if only he had the chance, but God took him too soon."

Mistakes? What was she talking about? "I'm not sure what you're saying, Mrs McIver? Your husband and this man were friends? *More* than friends?"

"They weren't anything," she snapped. "He was nothing but a demon. A devil. A disgusting sinner."

The pieces of the story were starting to form together in Ryan's mind.

He softened his tone and addressed the boy again. "Was that what you meant when you told your mother to stop lying on the television show last night?"

Simon nodded. "She always makes out like everything was so perfect, when it wasn't. It had all gone bad *before* he died."

Ryan gave him a smile of sympathy. "Okay, thank you, Simon, and you, too, Martha. You can go back to your rooms now."

Both kids vanished again, relieved to be out of there.

Ryan turned his attention back to the mother.

"Correct me if I'm mistaken, but from this I'm gathering that your husband left you for a man, and when your husband was in the accident, this man came to the hospital and wanted to see him, but you wouldn't let him. He believed he deserved to have some kind of say about what was going to happen with your husband's body and his organs. So, this must have been a serious relationship then, for him to think such a thing. Someone who was just having a fling or an affair wouldn't have believed they'd get to have say in the end of their lover's life."

"Don't use that word," she cried. "They weren't lovers. There was no love involved. I told you already, he was a devil and a sinner, come to tempt one of God's servants from the path of righteousness. That man didn't have a heart, or he would never have taken a loving husband and father away from his family."

"Why would you go on television when you have this kind of history?" Mallory asked. "Weren't you worried about the truth coming out?"

"I spoke the truth!" She was almost shouting now. "Our lives were the truth! Who he was before this demon came into our lives to tempt him away was the truth. I wanted the world to know what a good man he was, how he continued to help people, even after he died. I didn't want the final sin he committed to be what was remembered about him."

Ryan sat back. "So, others knew about the affair?"

She sniffed. "No, I don't think so, but I was frightened it would come out. I thought that if I made more noise than that evil creature did, that I would be able to drown out the disgusting things he was saying."

"Is it possible this man is the person who murdered Logan Foss?"

She shook her head. "I don't know. But once a sinner, always a sinner."

Ryan didn't believe in sin, and he certainly didn't share her beliefs in gay relationships being wrong in any way. He understood her pain, however. A marriage breaking down, no matter what the circumstances were behind it, was always painful. It was clear she blamed the other man rather than her husband, and he understood that, too. It was easier to blame someone else than think badly of someone you loved, especially when that someone was placed so high on a pedestal of supposed morality.

"We need to find out the identity of this man. Do you still have your husband's phone?"

"No, I don't. It was destroyed in the car accident."

"Do you know if he used any kind of cloud backup for photographs or anything like that?"

"He really wasn't into technology, Detective."

"So, you weren't able to go through his old photos after he died?"

Her jaw tensed. "If you think I'd have kept any photographs of that *man* who led him onto the Devil's path, you are very much mistaken."

How long did the phone company keep records for after someone had died? He'd have to get one of his team to chase them up.

Ryan pushed on. "What about a computer? Did he have a laptop?"

She shook her head. "We have a family PC which we all have to use, even the children for homework. We're not one of those families who spends all their time apart in different bedrooms while we all stare down at our phones. The computer is used for work, and that's all."

Ryan wondered how true that had been. If her husband had been sneaky enough to conduct an affair with another man, he might well have had another phone.

Was Ryan even on the right track? It was possible this mystery man had nothing to do with Logan Foss's death whatsoever. But the fact was that the man had clearly been upset—enough that security had been called at the hospital. Then, after the identity of one of the people who'd received one of Gregory's organs had been revealed on television, they'd been killed, and the organ had been removed. It did give them motive.

Clare suddenly reached out and grabbed his hand, tight enough to hurt. "Please, don't go around asking people about the affair," she begged. "I couldn't bear it if everyone knew."

Ryan untangled his hand from hers. "I'm sorry, but I don't have much choice. We need to find out the identity of this man. If you have any knowledge that can help us track him down, I suggest you tell us now, and then, assuming we're able to find him from that information, we won't need to ask many others."

She closed her eyes briefly and shook her head, but she started talking. "My husband didn't have many friends—didn't have *any* really. His life was all about us, his family, and his parishioners, and of course, God."

"Do you know where he might have met this man?"

"No, I have no idea." She wiped tears from her face. "It completely came out of the blue. I hadn't suspected a thing. I trusted him completely—why wouldn't I? He'd never given me any reason not to. I suppose I had noticed that he'd been going out a little more in the evenings, and had been taking calls more, but he always said it was to do with work, and I believed him."

"When did this start?" Ryan asked.

She closed her eyes briefly. "Months before he died."

"How many months?"

"Maybe six," she muttered.

"And how long before he finally left?"

"Two months before he died, but he didn't want anyone to know, either. The house comes with his job, so if his employers had found out, we'd have lost it, too. He didn't want us to end up homeless."

"But you must have known where he was living? The children must have known?"

She blinked away more tears and turned her face away. "I wouldn't let him see them. I wouldn't even let him speak to them. He waited outside the house a couple of times, and I told them the Devil had got him and that if they spoke to him, they'd open up their souls to the corruption of the Devil as well."

"You mean none of you had spoken to him in the months before he died?"

"No, we didn't."

"But when he was in the accident, the emergency services called you?"

"Yes. I don't know how or why. I guess he must have still had me down as his emergency contact."

"And you didn't contact his..." Ryan was about to say lover again and caught himself. "Friend."

He didn't want to ostracise her again when she was finally opening up.

"I already told you. I didn't know how. I have no idea how he found out about the accident, but he did."

It was a tragic story, for a man who was a vicar and who had clearly struggled with his sexuality, perhaps had married, and had children as a way of lying to himself. Then had finally made what must have been a very difficult decision to leave, only to have his estranged wife poison his children against him. But there was pain from his wife's side, too, and while Ryan didn't agree with what she'd done, he understood why. But for her to have not allowed the children to see their father was completely wrong, and then for him to have died without ever reconciling with them would be something they'd never forget. He couldn't imagine how damaging that was going to be for them in the long run.

"Okay, Mrs McIver. We'll leave it there."

They were going to have to ask questions—of the neighbours at his old vicarage house, and of his parishioners, and anyone else who might have known him. No matter how hard Gregory McIver's wife had worked to keep this secret, it was all going to come out.

# Chapter Twenty-Eight

Tova hadn't slept the previous night.

The mysterious driver of car that had sat behind her when her own had broken down had freaked her out. Even after she'd managed to get to bed, she'd spent the rest of the night lying there, frozen, her ears picking up on every tiny sound, her mind overanalysing what their origin might be.

Her thoughts had drifted to the handsome detective who had come to her rescue. If only she'd persuaded him to come home with her. She didn't even mean it in a romantic sense either—though she wouldn't have turned him down if he'd tried something—but more that she wished she could have positioned him on guard outside her door.

She'd given herself the morning off. She needed to take part in a little self-care and promised herself she'd stay off the internet and spend a few hours reading a trashy novel and eating chocolate.

Her phone rang, and she glanced down at the screen.

To her surprise, it showed her grandmother's number. Marjory never called her. Tova had bought her the phone because she'd hoped she might be able to video call her grandmother on the odd occasion that she wasn't able to get away from work, but despite having run Marjory though how it worked multiple times, she'd never quite got the hang of it. It was understandable, since she was in her nineties, but that was why Tova was so surprised now to see her grandmother's name on the screen.

Tova swiped to answer. "Nonna? How lovely to hear from you."

No reply came.

"Nonna?"

She listened carefully. Could she hear anyone there?

Marjory?" she said, using her grandmother's name and hardening her tone. "Marjory, if you're there, can you say something, please? Are you okay? Are you hurt?"

Worry spiked through her, shooting her veins full of adrenaline. What if her grandmother had fallen and the only way she'd been able to get help was by grabbing the mobile phone?

"Nonna, if you can hear me and you're hurt, you need to hang up and call nine-nine-nine, okay? Or can you get to the call button and get the attention of one of the staff?"

How far away were the care staff? How often did they go around and check on the residents? She pictured her grandmother lying on the floor, hurt and unable to get help.

Listening harder, she was sure she could hear breathing. It wasn't the breathing of an elderly lady who was frightened or hurt. It was slow and deep and deliberate, as though whoever was breathing wanted to be heard.

Tova froze. Chills ran across her skin.

"Hello? Who is this?"

Still, no response came.

"Why do you have my grandmother's phone?"

Had someone broken into Marjory's room and stolen it? How had they got into her room? What if they'd hurt Marjory at the same time?

Tova did her best to sound angry rather that scared. "Who is this? Are you the same person who left me that card and graffitied my car?"

Deep down, she was sure it was.

Still, whoever was on the end of the line said nothing.

She wanted to hang up, but at the same time she finally felt like she had a connection with the person who'd been tormenting her for the past few days, and she didn't want to let that go. She wanted to reach down the phone and grab them by the scruff and shake them and scream 'why' in their face. It was a man, she was sure of it. That was the breathing of a male.

But in the end, her concern for her grandmother won out over her need to learn who this was.

"I'm hanging up now," she said. "Do you hear me. I'm calling the care home to check on Marjory and then I'm calling the police."

She ended the call then swiped the screen for the number for her grandmother's home. A part of her was poised for the phone to start to ring again, and Marjory's name to pop back up, but it didn't happen.

She hit 'call', and the phone began to ring.

Tova grabbed her bag and hurried out to her car, the phone clamped between her shoulder and ear as she rummaged for her car keys. Her hands trembled, and her stomach felt weak. The world around her didn't quite feel stable, as though everything might break loose and float up around her at any moment.

"Park View Care Home," a bright female voice chirped.

"It's Tova Lane, Marjory's granddaughter. I've just had a call from her mobile, but it wasn't her on the end of the line. It sounded like a man."

"Oh...umm. Okay?"

She clearly didn't understand what Tova was trying to say.

"Someone—a strange man—has the phone."

Understanding dawned in the woman's tone. "That's right, she did have a visitor. A middle-aged man. A nephew, I believe."

Tova stiffened. "She doesn't have a nephew. I'm her only family."

"We've never been told not to admit any other family. We had no reason not to believe him."

"Maybe because he was trying to gain access to my grandmother's room to steal from her, or even worse. Can you go and check on her, please? Right away."

"I don't need to check on her."

"Yes, you do. She could be—"

"Ms Lane," the woman interrupted. "I don't need to check on her because I'm looking right at her. She's sitting in the day room having a cup of tea. She's fine."

Tova came to a halt and found herself having to bend over, one hand on her knee, her head hung, to stop herself passing out with relief.

*Oh, thank God.*

The images she'd had of her grandmother beaten half to death and some strange, threatening man looming over her with the phone Tova had bought her in one hand eased from her mind. The air left her lungs in a big whoosh.

She tried to make sense of what was happening.

Maybe no one had been in Marjory's room. She might have taken the phone out for some reason and someone else picked it up and called her number because hers was the only one programmed into it. Once more, was she reading something threatening into an event that could have been perfectly innocent.

But then why hadn't they said anything when they'd called? And who was the 'nephew' who'd been to visit Marjory?

Tova knew she wouldn't feel better until she'd seen her grandmother safe and well.

She became aware of the voice on the end of the line. "Hello? Ms Lane? Are you there?"

"Yes, sorry. Okay, that's good. I'm still coming over, though."

"That's fine, Ms Lane. We'll see you soon."

Tova ended the call and threw her phone back into her bag. She reached her car and pressed the fob to unlock it and got behind the wheel. She forced herself to take a couple of calming breaths. She wouldn't help anyone if she caused an accident because she wasn't concentrating on the road.

The drive to the care home only took about fifteen minutes. Tova pulled into the car park, eyeing each of the vehicles parked there, watching out for anyone suspicious. She wasn't completely sure who she thought she was going to see—some bulky man with a hood hiding his face, brandishing her grandmother's mobile phone—but everything seemed normal.

Still feeling unsafe, she got out and carefully locked the car behind her, checking it once, and then again to make sure. Her imagination was running away with her, but she didn't want to be one of those women who got back into her vehicle only to find some lunatic hidden on the back seat.

She trotted up to the entrance of the home and pressed the intercom. "Tova Lane to see Marjory."

Whoever had taken her nonna's phone must have had to do the same thing. Had it been this mysterious nephew?

The door buzzed open, and Tova pushed through into the reception area.

"She's still in the day room, Ms Lane," the woman on reception said.

Tova remembered her name was Susie. Susie nodded at the open door to where the light, airy day room contained high-backed chairs arranged in a semi-circle. They were all pointed towards the television, but no one was really watching it. Marjory was talking to the elderly lady sitting next to her and hadn't yet noticed her granddaughter was here.

Tova turned back to Susie. "On the phone, you said someone who called himself her nephew came to visit her."

"Yes, that's right."

"Did you get a name?"

Susie appeared to think for a moment. "Oh, he signed the visitor's book. Look, right here." She dragged the heavy book over and stabbed her finger at a name. "Do you recognise it?"

"John Doherty," she read and shook her head. "No, I don't."

There was no sign-out time next to the name, though the sign-in time was about ten minutes before Tova had received the phone call. Did that mean the man remained in the building, or was it more likely that he'd simply slipped out without bothering to sign the book again?

"Did you see him leave?" she asked.

"No, sorry, I didn't."

"Then he could potentially still be in Marjory's room."

Susie shook her head. "No, we checked the room after you'd called. No one was in there."

"What did he look like? Have you got cameras in here?"

Tova glanced up at the corners of the room to see blinking red lights.

"Yes, we have."

"I want to see the footage."

Susie winced. "Umm, I'd really have to check with my manager."

"That's fine." Tova straightened her shoulders. "Get your manager on the phone. I'd be more than happy to speak to him, too."

"It's actually his day off today."

"Then disturb him. You know how to get hold of me. I want to hear from him asap. Remind him that I work for the media and I'm sure he wouldn't like the press finding out that this care home allows random strange men to go into the room of vulnerable ninety-six-year-old women."

She didn't like to use her status on people, but sometimes it felt as though she was left with no other choice. And right now, she was genuinely worried, not only for her own safety but that of her grandmother, and she'd pull whatever strings she had to.

Susie paled. "No, of course not. I'll make sure he gets back to you as soon as possible."

"Thank you. I'm going to go and take a look in her room now."

Tova left the reception desk and made her way down the corridor to her grandmother's room. The brief flash of anger was once more replaced with nerves. What if the staff hadn't checked properly? What if the strange man had hidden in a different room and then slipped back in after the nursing staff had gone again? Maybe she should have brought someone else with her?

She stopped outside her grandmother's bedroom door and reached her shaking fingers to the handle. Tova was a strong, independent woman. She hated feeling like this. Whoever this person was, they were eroding at her confidence, chipping away at how she saw her place in the world.

Sucking in a breath, she threw open the door. The room wasn't large—enough to house her grandmother's double bed, a chest of drawers, and a dressing table. There was also a built-in wardrobe, and to the other side of it was a small en suite with a walk-in shower. Tova eyed both the wardrobe and the bathroom suspiciously. Could the man be hidden in one of those? The only way she'd find out was by checking.

A few long strides brought her to the wardrobe, and she threw open the door. Only her grandmother's shoes and dresses and coats greeted her. Just to be sure, she rifled through them anyway, making sure no one was hidden between their folds. It was empty. She quickly checked the bathroom, too, though there wasn't anywhere someone could hide.

She cast her gaze over the rest of the room, and it landed on an item on Marjory's dressing table.

The phone.

Tova picked it up. The phone wasn't locked—Marjory struggled enough learning how to use it without remembering to try to unlock it first—and so she was able to open it right away. She scrolled to the last number called. Sure enough, it was her number, made at the same time Tova had received the call.

Someone had definitely been in Marjory's room. Even if they hadn't taken the phone from her room and had found it somewhere else, they'd put it back in here.

She slipped the phone into her bag and went back out to the day room. Her grandmother was still in the same seat, and Tova crossed the room, forcing a smile to her face, as though everything was fine, even though it felt very far from being normal.

Her grandmother's expression brightened. "Tova. What a lovely surprise. I didn't know you were coming today."

"I was passing, Nonna, and I thought I'd drop in." She leaned down and kissed her cheek. "I hear you've been busy with visitors today."

Marjory's brow furrowed. "Yes, that's right. I have rather."

"Who was the man who came to see you?"

"My nephew. Daisy's son."

A fresh bubble of anger swelled inside her. Daisy had been Nonna's sister, but she'd died twenty years ago. Who was this man, and how did he know that about her?

"She never had a son, Nonna, remember? She didn't have any children, and even if she had, your nephew would be an old man by now."

"Didn't she? I'm sure that's who he said he was." She started to get distressed, wringing her hands.

Tova was worried she would damage her frail, papery skin, and took both her hands in her own to stop her.

"It's okay, don't worry. It doesn't matter."

Would there be cameras in the car park? Had the man even arrived by car? If so, they might have got the number plate. Something else occurred to her. If the man hadn't been wearing gloves when he'd placed the call, the phone would have fingerprints on it.

"Shit."

She'd touched the phone as well. Had she ruined them? Maybe, but it was all still evidence.

Tova had to stop herself. Evidence of what, exactly? That someone had called her? Just like with the thank-you card, it was hardly a crime.

Even so, this felt like it was escalating, though to what, she had no idea.

# Chapter Twenty-Nine

Macie left her house and shut the door behind her.
She hoped no one was going to recognise her after last night. Her Instagram account had blown up with a slew of comments and messages about the show, and she wanted to get away from everything online. She hadn't even taken her phone with her, happy to leave it switched off in her bedroom. Some of the messages she'd received had been crazy. It wasn't as though she'd said or done anything that could upset someone else, but still people—mainly men—had sent her obscene messages, calling her a bitch and a whore, and telling her what they'd like to do to her. Some of them were clearly using fake accounts, but plenty weren't.

The team at *Tova's Questions* had warned her this kind of thing would happen, but the sheer volume and hatred of the messages had shocked her. She hadn't told her parents about them, knowing how upset they would be.

She decided to go for a walk in the park and get some fresh air in her lungs. The torrential rain from last night had finally eased off, and though the ground was wet and the wind cold, it felt good to connect with nature. The park was almost empty, just a few dog walkers with coat collars turned up against the chill strode through the green space.

"Macie?"

A male voice called her name, and her heart sank. She hoped it wasn't going to be someone who recognised her from the show. Even worse, that it might be one of the trolls, but this time in real life.

She turned and breathed a sigh of relief. She did know them from the show, but not as she'd feared.

"Oh, hello," she said. "What are you doing here?"

The man smiled. "Taking a walk. How about you?"

"Same."

They smiled at each other awkwardly, and then he said, "I'm so pleased to bump into you. I felt we needed to have a catch-up after last night. I'm sorry things didn't quite go to plan. I hope you're feeling okay this morning."

"Yes, I'm fine, thank you. It was the McIver family I felt sorry for."

"Me, too. I'm actually putting something together for them and wondered if you'd like to be involved. Are you busy now?"

Macie glanced around. "Oh, well, I was just going to have that walk."

He raised his eyebrows hopefully. "Can it wait? I can drop you back soon?"

She nipped at the inside of her lower lip. "Umm...I guess so."

"It really would mean a lot."

She didn't feel she could really say no. "Sure, why not."

"Great. I'm parked this way."

She hugged her coat tighter around her body and followed him back through the park to the adjacent road.

"You know we've met before, don't you?" he said.

He surprised her. "What? Before last night?"

"Yes."

He had seemed familiar to her when they'd first met, but she'd put that down to the show. She angled her head towards him as they walked, studied his profile, and a flicker of recognition sparked in her memory.

"That night, at the hospital," she said, amazed, "after I got the call to come in because a donor had been found. I didn't have enough change for the car park, and you helped me out."

He nodded. "That's right."

It came back to her in a rush of recollection, the images from that night playing in a rolling film in her head. She'd been spinning with adrenaline and fear and anxiety and hope, unable to put a thought straight. There had been such a rush when she'd got the call, dizzying anticipation on top of the terror of having a major operation that she might not wake up from. Macie and her parents had left without thinking about needing money for the car park—hadn't even remembered a wallet—just the bag she'd had packed like an expectant mother in case the call came in. And it had. It had that night, and they'd raced to the hospital, completely forgetting about needing a ticket, and they'd ended up rifling through the car in the hope of finding some change in the glove box or dropped down the back of the seat. She'd been so upset, thinking she was either going to need to go in on her own, or else they'd both have to drive back to the house, but then this man—the same one standing before her right now—had asked if everything was all right, and she'd explained.

"You were upset that night, too," she remembered. His face had been streaked with tears and his eyes red.

"Yes, I was."

"But you still helped me." He'd found some change and given it to her, refusing her offer of taking his details so she could get it back to him. "Thank you for that. It meant a lot."

A muscle in his jaw twitched. "I hadn't known the reason you were there at the time."

She frowned over at him. "Why were *you* there?"

"Oh, just visiting someone."

"I hope they're better now."

He didn't reply but gestured to the road ahead. "That's my car," he said, nodding at a dark-grey Mazda sedan.

"Right."

He hit a button on a key fob to unlock it and then went to the passenger side to open her door for her. It struck her as a strangely old-fashioned gesture, but she smiled her thanks.

As she bent to get into the car, something hard and heavy cracked around the back of her head. The noise sounded as though her skull had fractured. She felt herself tilting forward, white sparks exploding in her vision. Strong, male hands caught her and slid her onto the passenger seat.

And then everything went dark.

# Chapter Thirty

Ryan called everyone together in the briefing room and filled his team in on what they'd learned from Clare McIver.

"We're looking for a man who was in considerable distress over the death of his lover, Gregory McIver. A man who was shut out by the family who had rejected Gregory, and who were now literally making life-changing decisions without his partner's involvement."

"They were never divorced or even officially separated," Mallory said, "so his wife did have the right to make those choices."

Ryan shrugged. "Something being legal doesn't change how the heart feels, it doesn't lessen the grief. It might have been enough to tip him over the edge and potentially murder one of the recipients of Gregory McIver's organs, Logan Foss."

DC Linda Quinn spoke up. "Do we really think this man might be responsible for killing Logan Foss? It wasn't as though Logan was to blame for Gregory dying or him being shut out of the family."

"Sometimes these things aren't always logical and, right now, it's the strongest lead we have." He looked around at the rest of his team. "We need to dig deep on this. I don't believe Gregory McIver kept everything a complete secret. He must have registered the address he was living at somewhere, on a phone statement, or with a bank, or even a store card company. Check with his work. Find out what address they had registered for him."

"Clare McIver said everything was kept a complete secret," Mallory said.

"*She* kept things a secret, but that doesn't mean Gregory's lover did. It sounds to me as though he wanted a legitimate place in Gregory's life, so maybe he registered a utility bill or a bank account in both of their names. If we can find out who he is and his address, we can get a search warrant for his home and his car. Something tells me we'll find substantial evidence, maybe the lost trainer or the murder weapon, there."

"What about the liver?" Dev asked from where he was sitting. "What would he have done with it?"

Ryan pursed his lips and shook his head. "Honestly, I have no idea."

A moment of silence fell over the room, each of the team considering what a broken-hearted man might do with his lover's liver.

Ryan wasn't sure it was something he wanted to dwell on, so he continued, "We have to consider that Gregory McIver didn't only donate his liver. I was able to speak to his consultant yesterday, and he informed me that Gregory donated several of his organs. Because he was what is known as a beating-heart organ donor, he was able to donate his heart, lungs, kidneys, liver, pancreas, and small bowel, among other things such as his corneas and inner ear. Are the other recipients potential victims as well?"

Mallory blew out a breath. "That's one hell of a paper trail we're going to have to chase. And what do we do with that information after we've got it? We could be looking at multiple people scattered all over the country. We don't have the resources to put police on each of them, and it would terrify them if we warned them, plus, surely we'd be breaking the anonymity of both the donor and the recipient?"

"The recipient, yes, but we already know the donor's family didn't want to stay anonymous in the first place. We know from the fact they've appeared on television shows that the family has no intention of remaining anonymous."

DC Shonda Dawson shook her head. "The recipients might feel differently, though. They might have gone out of their way not to learn who their organs came from, and if we approach them with this, we'll be ruining that for them."

Ryan shrugged. "I'd rather they knew than they ended up the same way as Logan Foss."

"There's one person who we know didn't want to stay anonymous," Mallory said. "The woman, Macie, who was on the show last night."

*Tova's Questions.* "Shit." Had the show just exposed Macie as being another recipient of Gregory McIver's organs? "You think she might be in danger?"

His sergeant nodded. "I think it's a possibility."

"We need to track her down and make sure she's safe. Have we got a recent address for her?"

"Yes, she's still living with her parents."

"Let's get someone round there, make sure everyone is okay."

# Chapter Thirty-One

Tova's phone rang, but she didn't recognise the number. After everything that had been happening recently, the thought of answering it made her anxious, but then she didn't want to ignore it either.

"Hello?"

"Ms Lane, it's Samuel Hall, the manager of your grandmother's care home."

She relaxed a fraction. "Oh, yes. Of course. Thank you for calling me back."

"I understand there was an incident this morning involving a visitor to the home."

"Yes, someone passed himself off as Marjory's nephew, only she doesn't have a nephew, and if she did, he'd be in his late sixties to early seventies right now and your staff said he was a younger man."

"That's right. A John Doherty." He paused and then asked, "You don't recognise the name at all then?"

Tova felt herself bristle. "Would we be having this conversation if I did?"

"No, I guess not."

"What I want from you, Mr Hall, is the security footage from your reception area, and any you might have from the car park around that time so I can get an image of the man. I'm in

227

contact with a detective who I can pass it on to, and hopefully we can figure out who he is."

His tone rose an octave. "You're in contact with the police? Don't you think that's a little extreme? After all, no actual harm was done."

"It's not just about the visit. I don't know if you're aware or not, but I do a television show—"

"Yes, *Tova's Questions*."

"That's right. Unfortunately, I've been dealing with a little...stalkerish behaviour from someone who is possibly a misguided fan, and the call from my grandmother's phone was just another episode in what has been a long line of incidents." She'd exaggerated slightly, but she wanted him to take it seriously.

"Oh, I'm so sorry to hear that."

She switched the phone to the other ear. "So, you can understand why it's so important that I figure out who is behind this, and if you could let your staff know that they shouldn't admit entrance to anyone claiming to be visiting my grandmother unless it's me, I would appreciate it."

"It's already been done."

"Thank you. I assume I can rely on you to get me that CCTV footage then?" She reeled off her email address. "I'll expect it imminently."

"I'll send it over as soon as I have it."

Tova ended the call. She chewed at the inside of her mouth, wondering whether she should call DI Chase again with this new information. She still had her grandmother's phone in her bag, which potentially might have this person's prints on it, and she remembered how he'd promised to run the thank-you card for prints as well. If they matched, it would at least prove that the same person was responsible for what was happening to her.

She paced her flat, trying to decide what to do. Maybe she should wait until she'd got the CCTV footage first, then she'd have something substantial to talk to the detective about. Receiving a strange phone call didn't feel like a big deal, but someone passing themselves off as her grandmother's nephew to get access to the care home did. She liked to think he might be impressed with her if she showed him her ability to investigate, just like he did. Of course, she wasn't a detective, but she was a journalist. She didn't want him to think of her as some helpless woman who always needed him to save her.

In the end, she distracted herself by making a cup of tea and scrolling through social media. She didn't stay online for long. She was still dealing with the fallout of last night's trainwreck of a show. What had the boy meant when he'd accused his mother of lying? Clare McIver was a God-fearing woman. Tova couldn't imagine what it was the boy thought she was lying about, and to announce it on television like that... What on earth had he been thinking? But then he was a teenager who had recently lost his father, and teens could be completely unpredictable.

Her email pinged, and she hurried to check it. As she'd hoped, it was from the care home manager.

Tova settled in her seat and opened up the attached security footage. "Let's see who you are then."

She hit 'play'. The footage wasn't great—greyscale and grainy. With the quality of easily accessible technology available today, and the amount of money she paid to the care home each month, she thought they could do with upgrading their cameras. She checked the time on-screen. It was a little before John Doherty had signed in the visitor's book. She hit fast forward.

Sure enough, a man was walking towards the reception desk. Tall and a little gangly, light-coloured hair. She frowned. What? No, it couldn't be...

What was *he* doing there?

She grabbed her phone and called the number. The phone rang and rang, and then the answerphone cut in.

"What were you doing at my grandmother's care home today?" she demanded. "Did you call me from her phone? What the hell is going on?"

Anger burned through her. She knew he wouldn't be in because of the late night they'd all had, but she knew where he lived.

# Chapter Thirty-Two

So far, they hadn't made any progress into finding out the identity of the man Gregory McIver had left his family for. Despite having left months before his death, Gregory hadn't registered any of his bills at a new address. The only reason Ryan could think for him not doing that was that he'd been protecting his estranged wife. Maybe he'd thought people would be less likely to ask difficult questions of her if his name was still appearing on all the post.

DC Craig Penn rushed up to his desk. "Boss, we've had a development. We sent a squad car around to Macie Ostrow's address. Her parents were home, but they said they haven't seen Macie since that morning. She went for a walk to the local park, but she didn't take her phone with her, which means we're unable to track it, and they haven't seen or heard from her since. They were already getting worried, and then uniform turning up has only confirmed that they might have a reason to be."

"Dammit," Ryan cursed.

"Do you think she's in danger?"

"I think it's a good possibility."

Ryan rose to his feet and lifted his voice to get the attention of the rest of his team. "Everyone, we need to consider Macie Ostrow as a missing person. Circulate a lookout on her, make sure everyone is aware that she's considered vulnerable. Let's get officers down to the park where she was last seen and trace the route she would have taken to get there. I want officers down at the park interviewing anyone who is around. Someone might have seen her."

"You think this man got her name from *Tova's Questions*," Mallory asked, "and he's tracked her down and taken her."

"Yes, I do. Finding her needs to be our number one priority. If we find Macie Ostrow, we find him as well."

"I'll check what CCTV we've got down there," Mallory said.

"We need to contact Macie's friends, see if anyone has heard from her. There is still a chance that she's simply gone for a coffee with someone and neglected to check in with her parents. After all, she is an adult."

Though this was a possibility, something in his gut told him that that situation wasn't what was happening here.

Ryan thought of something else. "There's one other person who's also been connected to each of these cases."

"Tova Lane," Mallory said.

"Exactly. She mentioned how she was getting those messages, remember? And last night she thought she was being followed by someone."

Mallory frowned. "She did?"

"Yes, she called me at midnight to say her car had broken down and there was someone in a car behind her, just sitting there. She was frightened. I sent a squad car to check up on her, but by the time they'd got to her, the car had already gone. Actually, I was going to check the ANPR cameras for that area to see if I could narrow down the number plate for the car. It was late, so there wasn't much traffic on the road."

He searched for one of his DCs and spotted him at his desk. "Dev, you were looking at the number plates for cars around the night Logan was murdered, weren't you?"

"That's right, boss."

"Can you cross-reference them with vehicles that were caught on a local ANPR camera around midnight last night."

"No problem."

Mallory was studying Ryan. "Do you think Tova Lane might be connected to the person who's doing this?"

"I do. I think she was right when she said the person who'd been sending her those messages was also the same person who'd killed Logan. What was it they'd asked her via the graffiti and in the thank-you card? Who's next? She suggested that it meant that they were asking who they were supposed to kill next, but when the guest of her next show was fine, it was assumed she was wrong. But it wasn't a general question. It wasn't about who was next on her show, it was about who would be revealed next as being one of Gregory McIver's donor recipients."

"We need to contact Tova then," Mallory said. "If she's unaware of this, she could be in danger."

"Or the killer somehow thinks she's an accomplice. That she's been unwittingly helping him pick out his next victim."

"Either way, we need to contact her. She might know who this person is."

"I completely agree."

He just hoped they weren't going to be too late.

# Chapter Thirty-Three

Tova hammered her fist on the door of his flat.

"I'm coming, I'm coming," he called from inside. "Don't break the door down."

It swung open, and she found herself staring into the face of her director, Emmett Callan.

"Do you want to tell me what you were doing at my grandmother's care home this morning?" She thrust out her phone with a screenshot of him standing at the reception desk.

He blinked at the picture and then looked up and, to her surprise, grinned. "Did you get it? John Doherty? John Doe?"

"Like an unidentified man?" she said, confused.

"Exactly. I knew you'd figure it out eventually. It's what makes you good at your job, this tenacity of yours. This inability to let things go."

"What? Figure what out? Why did you go to my grandmother's care home?"

"I remembered you telling me you'd given her a mobile phone and how frustrated you were that she hadn't been able to figure out how to use it."

She stared at him. "And so you thought you'd phone me from it? Why? It scared me."

"I wanted to get your attention, and it worked."

The things he was saying baffled her. "You could get my attention anytime. We work together."

He twisted his lips and shook his head. "Not about this. You know I couldn't talk to you at work about what we've been doing."

Her confusion deepened. "What we've been doing? I don't understand."

"Come in and I'll explain."

He backed out of the way to let her enter, and automatically, she stepped into the flat with him. She'd known Emmett for years and had been here plenty of times before when he'd had dinner parties. It had only been recently, after the death of a new boyfriend—who Tova had never met—that he'd become more withdrawn. It was understandable that he hadn't wanted to be sociable then. Grief could steal that from a person, as well as so much more.

Emmett moved past her, so they ended up doing a strange kind of dance in the hallway, and he put himself in front of the door. He reached out and clicked on the deadlock.

"We're in this together, you and I," he said, turning to face her. "You helped me find them, you're *still* helping me find them."

Her confusion morphed to discomfort. Maybe it would be better if he wasn't blocking the door like that. "What are you talking about?"

"I've just been trying to thank you, that's all."

She widened her eyes in understanding. "You were the one who left me that card? What about the other stuff? Did you graffiti my car?"

No wonder she hadn't thought about Emmett being down in the car park that day. He'd been right there the whole time, but she hadn't suspected a thing. She'd been worried about a stranger, not the person standing right beside her.

"Were you the one following me last night?" she asked.

"It was just a game. You don't need to take it the wrong way."

She stared at him. "You're crazy."

A strange noise came from somewhere deeper in the flat, and she glanced over her shoulder. *What is that?*

Emmett spoke again. "I thought you understood."

She focused her attention back on him. "Understood what?"

"About the loss I've suffered."

She blinked, her mind racing. "Your loss? Are you talking about your boyfriend dying?" She still had no idea what any of this had to do with her.

"Of course I am. I've been trying to make things right again. You know they took him from me."

"Who did?"

"His family. In those final moments, it was as though I didn't even exist. And then they tried to pretend Greg was something that he wasn't, like they could just erase a part of him that made him who he was."

Greg? He was talking about Gregory McIver. But the man had been married. He'd been a vicar, for goodness' sake. Was Emmett trying to say Greg hadn't been who he'd been made out to be? She remembered how his wife had been so insistent on telling the world what an incredible man her husband had been, how she'd shouted it from the rooftops. Had she done that to try to hide the truth, that actually her husband had been gay and had been in a relationship with another man before he'd died? Not that there was anything wrong with him being gay—with the exception that he'd been married and had a family of his own, and not with the person he'd apparently been sleeping with. She remembered the son, how he'd shouted at his mother to stop lying. Had the kids known as well? Had it been the perfect way for Clare McIver to recreate her memory of her dead husband, by trying to make him into the image of the man she'd wanted him to be and not the one he'd actually been?

Emmett's face had grown rigid, his hands clutched so tightly into fists that his knuckles were white.

She was sure she was only moments away from seeing blood drip from between his fingers from where his nails were surely cutting into his skin. She'd never seen this side of him. She, like the rest of the crew, had been aware that he'd been deeply affected by the loss of the man he'd called his partner a few months ago, but right now she wondered if it was something more than that. He seemed almost manic, like she was looking at the face of someone she didn't recognise.

That noise came again, like a cat crying or maybe a baby. What *was* that?

Emmett's voice drew her focus back to him. "You can help me find another one." His eyes brightened with a kind of mania.

"Another what?"

"Another one of the thieves who took Greg's organs."

Her stomach lurched. "What?"

"First Logan Foss. Then Macie Ostrow."

Had he been the one to kill Logan Foss? Surely not. The Emmett she knew wasn't capable of such a thing.

She took a step backwards. "Did you hurt Logan? What did you do to Macie?"

"Nothing yet. I thought you might want to help me."

"Help you what?"

"Take back what's mine."

Realising there was no escape behind her, she darted forward to try to get past him, but he was tall and lean, and he reached out and grabbed her arm. She opened her mouth to scream, but his hand clamped over it, cold fingers against her lips. She fought back, bucking and struggling, but he was frighteningly strong.

"Why are you being like this, Tova?"

He dragged her into the kitchen, and she discovered what the strange noise had been. Macie Ostrow was sitting on the floor, a gag in her mouth, her hands bound behind her and attached to the bars of a radiator.

# Chapter Thirty-Four

Ryan got off the phone just as Dev hurried up to his desk. "Boss, I did what you asked and compared the number plates."

"And?"

"I got a match. One of the cars we caught on an ANPR near the city centre last night has been matched to one of those caught on a speed camera a couple of miles from the warehouse."

Ryan straightened. "Excellent. Do we know who the car is registered to?

"Yes. His name is Emmett Callan. He works as a director on *Tova's Questions*."

"He's her director?"

Dev nodded. "Think about it. He would have known Logan Foss from the show. Maybe that's why Logan went with him willingly."

"Could he be the person who was arguing with Clare at the hospital?"

Dev raised his black eyebrows. "The one who didn't want the organs donated?"

"Shit." Understanding dawned on Ryan. "He wanted Gregory's organs back. He killed Logan Foss to get the liver and now he's possibly got Macie Ostrow for her heart."

Mallory joined the conversation. "Wait a minute. Wouldn't Clare have recognised Emmett when she did the show? Even if she hadn't met him before the night of Gregory's death, Emmett came to the hospital."

"The nurses and security staff wouldn't let him in the room, remember? Clare said she was too caught up in what was happening to her husband to go out and see what was causing the commotion. She said she never got a look at him, and she obviously hadn't been lying. Maybe if she had, he would never have got the chance to murder Logan." He turned to his DC again. "Have you run a background check on him?"

"He's clean. No priors. Not even a parking ticket?"

"We need to find him. Do we have a home address?"

"Absolutely. It was registered with the DVLA."

Something else occurred to him. *Tova.* Emmett had been following her that night. Was he the same person responsible for all the other things she'd reported as well? The card left on her doorstep and the graffiti? He'd said thank you, hadn't he? What would he be thanking her for if it wasn't for helping him?

Was there any possibility Tova Lane was involved in Logan Foss's murder? Or was she going to be the next victim?

"Has anyone managed to get hold of Tova Lane as well?" Ryan asked.

"I don't think so, boss."

Ryan remembered how she'd phoned his mobile. If he went back through his call log, he should have her number on there. He pulled it up and called the number. The phone rang and rang, and then the answerphone cut in.

Could Tova be in danger, too? He kicked himself. She'd told him about the letter and the graffiti and that someone had been following her, and he hadn't taken it seriously. What if she was dead now? Would he be, at least in part, to blame?

"What about Macie Ostrow?" he asked. "Any sign of her yet?"

"No. We've got uniform still searching."

"There's a possibility she might be with Emmett then, but whether that's against her will or not, it's impossible to say."

Linda stood from her desk. "Boss, we've got CCTV from near the park where Macie was last seen. She's with a man. It looks to be Emmett Callan."

That confirmed it. He wasn't going to wait a moment longer.

"We need to put a task force together to go to Emmett's flat. If he's there, he could well have Macie with him, and possibly even Tova Lane. He needs to be considered unstable and dangerous."

"Are we looking at a possible hostage situation here, boss?" Dev asked.

"Yes, I believe so."

He just hoped he could get everyone out alive.

# Chapter Thirty-Five

Tova's hands were bound in the same way Macie's had been, and Emmett had tied her to the metal leg of his breakfast bar. She'd tried to scream when he'd taken his hand off her mouth, so he'd stuffed a tea towel between her lips to keep her quiet. She wished she'd been able to fight him, but her small stature hadn't helped, and he'd easily overpowered her.

Across the room, Macie looked terrified. Tears streamed down her face. Tova tried to catch her eye to tell her everything would be all right, but she couldn't promise that. No one knew where they were, and no one had any reason to suspect Emmett. Unless someone else saw the footage from the care home and recognised him, but even then, they wouldn't have any reason to think that was connected to Logan Foss's murder.

She still couldn't get her head around what was going on. Gregory McIver had been Emmett's lover, and when he'd died, Emmett must have snapped and decided to track down the people who'd taken Gregory's organs and tried to get them back. Tova would never understand his rationalisation. It hadn't been Logan Foss's fault that he'd been given Gregory's liver, or Macie's fault that she'd got his heart.

What did Emmett think he was going to do with the organs when he got them all back?

It didn't bear thinking about.

Emmett paced back and forth. He was highly agitated, his hands in his hair, the muscles in his face twitching.

"You hurt me, Tova," he said. "I thought you and I were in this together, and then you act like it means nothing. I thought you understood."

Emmett had thought she was helping him.

Maybe she could make that work for her to get herself free and then help Macie. She couldn't just sit here while he did to Macie what he'd done to poor Logan.

Emmett continued to pace. "When you brought up the suggestion of doing a show on transplant recipients and the donor's family, at first, I thought it was accidental. It's your job, after all. But then the way you dug and dug, asking all the right questions, I started to wonder if there was more to it, and that you knew exactly what you were doing. Pointing me in the right direction. I know it's your job to investigate stories, and this definitely was a story. People loved it. They teared up with emotion at your work, fucking hypocrites. All they could see was the happiness of those who'd benefited instead of the heartbreak of those left behind. Oh, maybe they'd given people like me a fleeting thought, but really, all they wanted was the feel-good part of the story. They were just thankful they weren't the ones who'd been put in that position."

He shook his head as though in awe. "It made me wonder how much else you'd uncovered. Did you know about me? Did you know how I'd been treated as though I didn't even exist? No one had ever asked my opinion on what happened. They'd never taken my feelings into account, that maybe I didn't want that for Gregory, for his beautiful body to be butchered like that. How could they? How could they stand to know someone was doing that to him, after everything he'd been through? Hadn't he been hurt enough?"

A tear slipped down Emmett's cheek, and he swiped it away.

Despite everything, Tova found herself feeling sorry for him. It must have broken his heart to not be able to spend Gregory's final moments with him, and then for his family to act like he didn't exist. It didn't excuse what Emmett had done, however.

Emmett sniffed and continued. "All it did was confirm to me that they didn't really love him, not like I did. They made all the right noises, but they couldn't have for him to have ended up like that. I know Greg didn't love Clare. Not like that. Just because there was a piece of paper that gave her more rights than me, we were all supposed to abide by it.

"That hurt, Tova. Did you know that? I can't explain how much it hurt. They took something from me, and my opinions on it weren't even asked. No one understood, except for you, or at least I thought you understood, but I guess I was wrong about that, too."

Tova tried to speak against the gag.

He stopped pacing and faced her. "What are you saying?"

She tried again, but it was impossible to get the words out.

He leaned over her and tore the gag from her mouth.

Tova gasped for breath. "I do understand, Emmett. I do. I'm sorry."

"I don't believe you. Not now."

"You just frightened me because of my grandmother. I thought someone was going to hurt her."

His expression relaxed a fraction. Did he actually believe her? How the hell could he think she'd supported him in this? In actually murdering an innocent young man? He thought she'd gone out of her way to track down these people for him.

If she yelled for help, would someone hear her? She could try, but he was bound to just gag her again.

If she could talk her way out of these bonds, maybe she could grab one of the knives from the kitchen block. That would give them a better chance of escaping than if she just shouted and he gagged her again.

One thing Tova had always been good at was putting on an act.

# Chapter Thirty-Six

Macie had no idea what Tova Lane had done to deserve being tied up in here with her. She'd recognised the director from Tova's show. Had they somehow been in this together and things had gone wrong?

What was going to happen to her? Her parents would be wondering where she was by now, and they'd be worried. When would they report her missing? She didn't think it would take long. Even though she was an adult, they were overprotective of her because of her heart, and if they didn't know where she was and she didn't have her phone with her, they'd get worried fast.

The last person who'd been in this position had been killed. Logan Foss. He'd been on the television show before her, and he'd ended up dead.

Emmett was taking his grief out on the wrong people. She wasn't to blame. Logan Foss hadn't been to blame. The death of his partner, and his exclusion in his final moments—and even, she assumed, in his funeral—had tipped him over the edge. There was no reasoning with him. The only way she was going to get out of this was if she worked out a way to get free, or if her parents raised the alarm and the police were able to work out what had happened.

Across the room, Tova yanked against her bindings. Where Macie was terrified, Tova just looked furious. She was talking to Emmett now, trying to reason with him. Emmett seemed to believe that she had helped him track down the recipients of Gregory McIver's organs.

*Had* she been involved? It had been Tova's show that had lured Macie out in the open. Did Tova's anger stem from being stabbed in the back?

Silently, Macie sent up a prayer.

*Please, God, if I get out of this, I'll do better.*

She'd already been given one second chance. What was the possibility of her getting another?

What was Emmett planning? To kill her, she had no doubt. She was only surprised he hadn't done it already.

Tova appeared to be trying to reason with him.

"You should let me help," Tova said. "Wasn't that what you always wanted? A partner in this? What you thought you had?"

"You'd want to help kill her?" His tone was doubtful.

"Isn't that what all this has been about? All you have to do is untie me."

His lips thinned. "You're lying to me."

Tova's gaze flicked to the block of knives on the counter behind him. "No, I'm not."

He'd spotted where her line of sight had gone and turned to follow it.

*No,* Macie thought. *No, no, no.*

He reached out and drew the largest of the knives out of the block, the metal catching in the light.

Macie squealed and pushed herself back against the radiator, terror flooding like iced water through her veins.

Emmett approached Tova. "You've disappointed me, Tova. Just like everyone else, you've let me down."

She shook her head wildly. "No, Emmett, stop! Please!" He moved closer, and she let out a scream. "Help, someone help me."

"Enough!" he commanded and swooped down and drove the knife into her stomach.

Macie screamed against her gag. Oh God. She would be next.

Tova slumped back on the metal leg of the breakfast bar, her stomach growing steadily darker with blood. She wasn't moving.

Macie scraped the side of the gag against her shoulder. It seemed to have loosened. She used her tongue to push it from inside her mouth, and it gave further.

Emmett turned to face her. His eyes darkened with madness. "You want the gag off, huh? It won't do you much good. Even if you scream, no one will get here quickly enough to save you."

Maybe it was just that he was so desperately lonely that he wanted someone to talk to, but whatever the reason, he crossed the room and reached down to pull the gag from her mouth. She couldn't take her eyes off the knife held in one hand, the way the blood—Tova's blood—dripped from the point.

Macie found her voice. "Do-don't you want Gregory to live?"

Emmett jerked back. "He's not alive. That's the whole fucking point."

"But a piece of him is," she continued, "inside me. You can still feel his heart beating."

"It's not his heart anymore. You stole it. You stole a piece of him."

She shook her head. "No, it was given to me."

His fingers tightened around the handle. "It was given to you by someone who had no right to give it."

This wasn't going how she'd hoped.

"Just feel the beat. It was *his* heart. If you kill me, that beat will stop forever. It'll just be another piece of meat."

His chin trembled, and she could tell she'd affected him.

"Stop it!"

"Put your hand on my chest," she encouraged, though her voice trembled with terror. "Feel it for yourself. Feel the life."

He shook his head, his lips pinched. "It's not him."

"If it's not him, then why do you want to take it? It's not going to bring him back. It's not who he was, but a part of him can still live on."

Emmett hesitated but then lowered himself to his knees in front of her. The knife was still clutched in one hand, but he reached out with the other one and placed his palm to her chest.

"I can feel it beating." Tears spilled from his eyes.

He shifted position to bring himself lower and pressed his head to her chest, his ear above the place where her scar was located. His hair was right beneath her nose. She froze, staring down at the top of this man's head. He was a killer. He had murdered Logan and stabbed Tova and now he was lying here, practically in her lap, with a knife in one hand and his head against her chest.

She felt as though if she so much as breathed the wrong way, he'd stab her.

The sight of the woman bleeding out on the other side of the room terrified her, too. Though she was small in stature, something about Tova's presence had always made her seem so much larger. But now she was hurt—possibility mortally—Tova seemed tinier than ever, almost childlike. She'd stopped moving, and Macie couldn't see her chest rising and falling anymore. Was she dead?

Macie had never seen a dead body before. The sight horrified her. Was that going to be her soon?

The man lying against her continued to cry, his shoulders shaking. The knife he'd used to stab Tova hung loosely from his fingers. She wanted to do something, but with both hands still taped to the radiator, she was helpless. She could kick out at him or use her knees, but all that would do was make him angry.

Tears slipped down her face, and she twisted her head away and squeezed her eyes shut so she didn't have to look at either him or poor Tova. She'd have given anything to be back in her own home right now, in her own bed, with her mother asking her if she wanted anything, and then, even when she said no, bringing her a cup of tea anyway. She'd been so lucky, and she'd never appreciated it. Her life was far from perfect, and she'd been through so much, but she'd still been alive. She'd been able to enjoy those simple pleasures of a warm bed and loving parents and she'd thought she needed more. Maybe she would have needed more, in time, but right now, she'd give anything to go back to what she had.

A commotion came from outside. The roar of engines of multiple vehicles pulling up and people shouting things to one another.

She was fairly sure she knew the cause of the commotion. The police were here. They were here to help her. Were they too late for Tova, though? She didn't think the other woman was breathing, but it was hard to tell from this side of the room. The amount of blood on the floor around her was a gruesome sight, though.

The noise outside got his attention, and he lifted his head from her chest. She held her breath, her back pushed hard against the metal of the radiator bars, as though she might be able to vanish through them. What would he do if he thought the police were going to come in here? Would he just kill her?

Emmett got back to his feet. She opened her mouth to scream for help, but his hand clamped down over her lips, and that was quickly followed by the rip of fresh tape. His hand was replaced by more of the black tape he'd used to tie her up with, and her opportunity to let anyone know she was still alive in here vanished.

"Don't let me regret allowing that heart to continue to beat," he warned her.

He crossed the flat to look through the window to the street below while standing far enough back that he wouldn't be seen from outside.

Sudden fear filled her that the police being here had put her in more danger instead of less. He'd feel the need to finish what he'd planned now time was running out.

The police were in the building now, she could tell by the amount of movement that was coming from outside the door. What were they doing? Saving everyone else except her? Fresh tears swam in her eyes. They were evacuating the other residents. What did that mean? That they thought the other occupants might be in danger? Did they think he was armed, or were the police the ones who were coming in here with guns?

Emmett went to the front door and double-checked it was locked, then he looked around. His gaze landed on a large chest of drawers. He went over to it and lowered his shoulder to push it across the floor, blocking the doorway. He clearly didn't plan on either letting anyone in here or letting them leave either.

He wasn't going to allow the police to take him alive, she was sure of it. But would he take her down with him?

# Chapter Thirty-Seven

The evacuation on the block of flats was already in progress when Ryan arrived. They didn't know if Emmett Callan was armed with a gun, but it was a possibility. What they *did* know was that he was dangerous and that he'd already taken hostages. They couldn't risk him taking any others.

Uniformed police in bulletproof vests and protective helmets ushered out confused civilians of all ages and ethnicities. A young family carried a screaming baby while dragging a squalling toddler along. A group of students in their late teens and early twenties looked less worried and more thrilled at the excitement. An elderly couple left holding hands, an equally elderly dachshund waddling along on the end of a lead behind them.

The inhabitants of the flats would only have been told there was an incident, so now they'd be speculating about what was going on. Did they have a terrorist in their building? A bomb, perhaps?

The residents were led away, taken beyond the outer cordon to safety.

Several incident vans were parked up outside the street, blocking the road from anyone trying to drive down and also from anyone who might try to get away. An Armed Response Unit had also been called in. This was a dangerous man who'd killed before and could well have killed again, and Ryan wasn't going to take any chances.

The buildings around the flats also housed lots of different people. They were all interested in what was going on. He caught the glimpse of a couple of phones held up at windows and knew they'd end up on social media any minute now.

Would Emmett be paying much attention to social media? It was hard to say what he was doing right now. Ryan hadn't spotted any sign of him at the windows or, for that matter, any sign of the two women, but they'd run a trace on Tova Lane's phone and confirmed that she was in the building.

Ryan spotted Lars MacMahon, the Force Hostage Negotiator. Lars was in his fifties—a giant bear of a man who could probably squash most people flat but whose natural calm, gentle demeanour meant he would never do such a thing—or at least only when absolutely necessary.

"Lars, thank you for coming."

Lars jumped straight to business. "What do we know about him?"

"He's a white male, aged forty-seven, works as a director in a television studio. We believe he murdered a man and cut out his liver and took it with him. The liver belonged to his lover but was donated upon his death. We think he took it back."

"What about the hostages?"

"Potentially, two women are in there with him. Forty-two-year-old Tova Lane, and twenty-seven-year-old Macie Ostrow."

"Have we established the welfare of the hostages?"

Ryan shook his head. "Not yet."

"Do we think he means the women harm?"

"Yes, we believe so, if he hasn't hurt them already. We do have a mobile number for him."

Lars nodded. "Let's try it."

Ryan's need to control each situation meant he found it frustrating that he wasn't the one who'd be doing the negotiating, but that wasn't part of his job. He'd located Emmett Callan and he would make the arrest, but what mattered the most now was making sure the two women were kept safe and he was put behind bars.

Lars dialled the number. "It's ringing." He put it on speaker so Ryan could hear what was being said.

The flat was on the third floor at the front of the building, looking down onto the street. Ryan squinted up at the window, trying to get any sense of the people inside.

Would Emmett answer or just switch off the phone?

To Ryan's surprise, he answered.

"I know who this is. I don't want anything to do with the police."

"Emmett," Lars said, "can I call you Emmett?"

"That's my name," came the curt reply.

"My name is Lars MacMahon, and I'm here to make sure we can resolve things without any more lives being lost."

"Lives have already been lost."

Lars shot Ryan a look. "Are you talking about Tova and Macie?"

"No."

"So, the women are unharmed."

"That's not what I said."

Lars kept his tone calm. "Emmett, if you have injured people in there with you, let them go. We have paramedics on hand who can help them."

"There's only one life I ever cared about, and he's gone."

Lars craned his neck up at the flat window. "Are you talking about Gregory McIver? Do you think he would have wanted you to do this? He was a vicar, wasn't he? He believed in God and Heaven and Hell. What would he say to you right now?"

Emmett gave a cold laugh. "Yes, he believed in all that, but that doesn't mean I do. All his church and God ever did was repress him. He'd lived a lie almost his whole adult life. We wasted so many years, so many. And then when he finally was truthful about who he was, his so-called God stole him away from me again."

"Then your argument is with his God, not with the women you have in there. Let them go."

"I let them go and you'll just storm in here and arrest me. I'm not stupid."

"Then what do you want?" Lars said. "Tell us what we need to do for you to help us bring this to an end."

"I want you to bring my partner back."

"You know we can't do that. Nothing is going to do that, certainly not hurting those two women."

Emmett sniffed. "Macie has a piece of him inside her. A real, beating piece of him. It feels different to the other one. That was just meat. This feels alive."

Ryan understood what that meant. Macie Ostrow was alive—at least she was for the moment. A wrong move by them could change all that, however.

"All we want is for no one else to be hurt," Lars said. "Tell us how we can help you achieve that?"

"You can't."

Ryan caught sight of Mallory hurrying towards them. Like the rest of them, she was fully kitted out in protective gear. She jerked her head to get him to step away from Lars.

Mallory kept her voice low. "Boss, I spoke to a couple of the neighbours, and they've reported hearing screams."

"How long ago?"

"About fifteen minutes. Not long before we arrived."

The news worried Ryan. They might not have time for this. "So someone might be hurt, or worse."

"It's a possibility."

"Damn it. Have we got the drone yet?"

She nodded. "It's coming."

The high-pitched buzzing of the drone came from above them. The camera fitted on the front of the equipment would give them a view into the flat. Ryan hoped Emmett wouldn't notice. The noise from all the vehicles and people outside would hopefully disguise the whine of the drone.

One of the team members controlling the drone called out, "We've got a woman on the floor, she's hurt. There's blood everywhere. She's not moving."

"Shit." Ryan turned to Lars, who hit the mute button. "We don't have time for further negotiations," Ryan said. "We need to get in there."

He hoped Emmett wouldn't see them coming and do something drastic. The lives of these women hung in the balance.

He gave the call for the Armed Response Unit to enter the building.

They ran up the stairs, the thunder of their footfall sounding like an army. A battering ram was produced at Emmett's front door, a couple of armed officers standing either side to make entry first.

Ryan and Mallory hung back, allowing them to do their job.

The door burst inwards, and the Armed Response Unit stormed the flat.

"Armed police! Freeze! Don't move a muscle."

Ryan wanted to get in there, but he needed to wait. He took up position in the hallway, Mallory close behind.

Another call came. "Female victim is down."

Shit. They were too late. Was it Tova or Macie? They needed to get paramedics in there, but they couldn't until the threat had been neutralised.

Ryan and Mallory gave them enough time to secure the area and then entered as well. Ryan took in the scene. The man was on the floor with the young woman, Macie, pulled partially in front of him, protecting his torso. Her hands were secured to the radiator behind them. Next to him was a knife covered in blood. On the other side of the room, he recognised the blonde hair of Tova Lane, but she was surrounded by a pool of blood and was unmoving.

Emmett's gaze flicked from the armed police who were standing over him, their weapons aimed, to the knife on the floor. Ryan could see it in his face, his determination to end things his way.

"Don't do it, Emmett," Ryan shouted.

The armed police wouldn't risk firing when there was such a great chance of hitting Macie.

Emmett shook his head. "What's the point. Macie is right. I can never bring him back. He's gone. Even that parts of him that keep beating aren't really him."

"It's not the fault of the people who received his organs. They're innocent."

"All I wanted was to be acknowledged. We loved each other, and he died, and I wasn't even allowed to hold his hand when he passed. Clare didn't want to admit to herself that he was who he was. He loved her, too, but not in that way, and she refused to accept it."

"You didn't take it out on her, though."

"He loved his children, more than anything else in the world. I wouldn't have taken their mother from them, not when they'd lost their father as well."

Ryan shook his head at him. "But you're happy taking the lives of innocent people."

"I wanted a part of him back again."

Ryan watched the decision settle across his features. Hope dying in his eyes.

"I'm sorry. I can't—" Emmett reached for the knife.

"Emmett!" Ryan yelled. "Stop!"

A loud crack cut through the air. Emmett jolted backwards like he'd been punched, and his whole body went rigid. Macie screamed.

A fast, repetitive volley of clicking filled the room.

The police hadn't risked a gunshot. They tased him instead.

The flat was filled with movement and shouting, police and paramedics rushing forward.

Emmett groaned. He wasn't dead, though he'd probably wished he was. The man he'd loved was gone, and he was going to be spending many, many years behind bars.

"We've got a pulse!" one of the paramedics said.

Tova was still alive, though hanging on by a thread.

Macie sobbed while police officers undid her hands from the tape and helped her to her feet. She clutched at them, as though she needed their support just to stay upright.

Mallory went to her and crouched to help.

Macie's line of sight was fixed on Tova. "Is she going to be okay?"

The paramedic looked over. "We're doing everything we can."

# Chapter Thirty-Eight

Ryan rubbed his hands over his eyes and shut his computer down. The amount of paperwork he'd been drowning under after the arrest of Emmett Callan had been ridiculous, and he was glad to have most of it done now.

The search of Emmett's flat had revealed enough evidence to put him away for the murder of Logan Foss. As well as the missing trainer, they'd also discovered Logan's liver in a sandwich bag in the freezer. The discovery was a macabre one, but even questioning Emmett hadn't revealed exactly what he'd planned to do with them once he'd collected all the others.

Both Macie and Tova had been taken to hospital. Macie had been shaken but otherwise unharmed, but Tova Lane was going to be in for a long recovery, if she survived her ordeal at all. Already, the papers and social media were flooded with the story and an outpouring of support for Tova. If nothing else, this would have done wonders for Tova's career.

Ryan stood from his desk to leave for the day, but a figure he didn't normally see in his office blocked the way.

"Townsend," he said in surprise. "I didn't expect to see you here."

"I know you've had a busy day, Ryan, but I'm afraid we need to have a chat about Cole Fielding's death."

Ryan's blood ran cold. Was this it? Had some evidence finally come to light to prove that he was on the bridge that night Cole had fallen? He'd been waiting for this moment for a long time, and a part of him was relieved. At least he'd know the truth now. He'd lose his job and most likely serve time—and being in prison when you were a police officer was never a good thing—but in a way it felt like a cleansing.

"No problem. Take a seat." Ryan gestured for Townsend to take his chair, and he pulled one over from another desk. "How can I help?"

"The post-mortem has come back on Cole, and the result was inconclusive, though some fibres were found in his lungs."

"What sort of fibres."

"They're believed to be the same ones used for the sheets and pillows in the hospital."

"So, is that unusual? He was in the hospital for a long time. It would make sense that he might have inhaled some of the fibres."

"That's true, but we still have to make some enquiries. One of the nurses mentioned that another of our police officers had been in to speak to Cole a few months ago, not long after he'd regained consciousness, but we didn't have any record of that happening. Then I remembered how I'd called you to let you know that Cole had regained consciousness. Did you go and see him that day, Ryan? You need to be truthful with me. There are CCTV cameras that I can easily check to find out if you're lying, and it'll look worse on you if you are."

Ryan had no choice but to admit it. "Yes, I went to see him. I was only there for a couple of minutes, and then I left."

"Why did you go and see him?"

"Because I wanted to know what state he was in. I couldn't stand the thought that he'd recovered and would be walking around as though nothing had ever happened."

Townsend's eyes narrowed. "Couldn't stand the thought enough to make sure that never happened?"

Ryan bit down hard enough on his lower lip to hurt. "What are you trying to say here, Townsend? Are you accusing me of finishing off Cole? If so, I suggest you come back with some proof. You said yourself, there are CCTV cameras. Go and check the footage. If you find me on any of them on the night Cole died, you can come back here and arrest me. But right now, Cole Fielding is just a case of an unexplained death that is most likely the result of his long illness and brain injury."

That was most likely the case, but Ryan still hadn't been able to bring himself to come right out and say that he had nothing to do with Cole's sudden demise. He wasn't going to tell him that he'd been drinking that night because of a fight with his ex-wife, and that he didn't have any memory of that time.

Townsend would have to check the CCTV now, and if it happened that Ryan was on it after his recent drinking session, Ryan would have to put his hands up. He wanted to think he didn't have it in him to take another person's life, but deep down he knew that wasn't true. After all, he'd seriously considered the possibility that he'd been the one who'd put Cole in hospital in the first place. And that day in the courtroom, when Cole had laughed at them, Ryan had wanted to climb across the benches and everyone who stood in his way and wrap his hands around Cole's throat and choke the life out of him.

"Are we really going to waste time and resources on someone like Cole Fielding?" Ryan said. "He was gravely ill, so it's not as though his death was that unexpected, was it?"

"You're right, it's not, but Cole served his time for what he did, and he needs to be treated like any other member of the public."

Ryan couldn't help but snort his derision. "Served his time? What time? Certainly wasn't anything like the seventy or more years that he stole from Hayley or the forty-plus years Donna and I might have had with her."

"No, I know that, Ryan. And I'm sorry, I really am."

"Yet you're still here, questioning me about his death."

He discovered the anger still existed inside him, as hot and bright as it had ever been. Only now there was no one to direct the anger towards. Cole Fielding was dead. Should he direct it towards the judge who'd given him such a short sentence, or the pub that had continued to serve Cole alcohol, even though he'd clearly been drunk, or the makers of the car Cole had been driving when he'd mowed down Hayley? He knew none of these were truly responsible for what had happened, but the thought of suddenly no longer having anywhere to aim his fury made him feel like a drowning man in the middle of an ocean with no life raft to cling on to.

He glanced down to find his fingers tapping against his thigh. He squeezed his hand shut. He'd been better recently—not keeping himself awake at night because he'd been checking his doors and windows over and over until he could sleep. There were still die-hard habits such as keeping his desk in exactly the right order or making sure his food was at correct positions on his plate, but the grip on him had eased.

"It was just a question, Ryan. You know I had to ask it. It's procedure."

He forced himself to refocus on DS Townsend. "Right, well, if there aren't any other questions, I'd like to get on now. It's been a busy day."

Townsend cleared his throat. "I hope Cole's death will at least bring you some kind of peace, Ryan."

"Me, too," Ryan said, though he wasn't holding on to much hope.

Townsend nodded. "I'll be in touch." His expression softened a fraction. "I don't think any of us would have blamed you, off the record."

"Blamed me?"

"If you had killed that son of a bitch. He didn't deserve to live."

He saw DS Townsend out and then realised he needed to call Donna. Would she even pick up after the scene he'd caused at her place? He wasn't sure what he'd do if that dickhead picked up the phone instead. He closed his eyes briefly. It wasn't any of his business who Donna saw. They were divorced now, and she'd beaten cancer and had her life ahead of her once more. It just made him furious that the creep could come crawling back now all the messy stuff was done, and that she'd allow him back into her life. Donna deserved so much better than what that prick could give her.

Better than Ryan had ever given her as well.

With a sigh, he picked up the phone and called her number.

"Ryan?" she answered, her tone cool.

"I have to tell you something, Donna. It has nothing to do with the dickhead, okay?"

Her tone grew chillier. "You know that's none of your business."

"I know, that's why I'm not calling you about it. Listen to me. Cole Fielding is dead."

He heard the breath rush from her lungs and the faint thud as she dropped to a chair.

"What?"

"He's dead, Donna. Died in his sleep, apparently, though I believe the post-mortem came back as undetermined."

"Undetermined?" she said after a moment's silence. "So, they don't know what killed him?"

"It's not clear, but obviously, he'd been sick for some time. I think the main thing that's causing the confusion is that the doctors thought he was getting better and so they weren't expecting him to die so suddenly, but the pathologist found some fibres in his lungs, too, which has given cause for doubt."

"What kind of fibres?"

"From the hospital sheets."

"What does that mean?"

He chose his words carefully. "I guess they're wondering if someone might have smothered him."

She paused on the end of the line. "*Did* someone smother him?"

"Not to my knowledge," he answered truthfully.

She let out a sigh. "I'm not going to pretend that I'm not happy he's dead. I hated to think of him having a place in this world when Hayley didn't."

"I know. I feel the same way."

They both fell silent, joined together in remembering the daughter they'd had stolen from them.

"Well, I'd better get on," he said.

"Thanks for letting me know, Ryan."

"Of course."

He ended the call and sat back down and rearranged the contents of his desk.

# Chapter Thirty-Nine

Macie blocked another idiot on social media and tossed her phone to one side. She'd found herself caring less about people leaving horrible comments and sending her threatening messages. She told herself it was more important that she cared about the people she touched than the ones who just wanted to troll her.

There had been a while after the kidnapping where she'd considered shutting herself off from social media altogether. Things had been bad after the police had rescued her from Emmett and people had caught her face on camera and posted it online. But then she decided she wasn't going to let the fuckers win. Her life had already been made smaller because of her heart problems, and she wasn't going to cut herself off from people even more because of them.

Her mother's shout came from downstairs. "Macie, dinner!"

Macie smiled to herself. It was her favourite—baked ham and mash. Her mother was spoiling her, but now Macie was letting her and doing so without being smothered by guilt.

She'd been given two second chances now, and she wasn't going to spend the gift she'd been given by moping around and feeling sorry for herself. Maybe she'd never be climbing mountains or running marathons and raising huge amounts of money for charity, but she could live her quiet life and be happy.

She put her hand to the scar on her chest. The details of Gregory McIver's story had come out, and she felt nothing but sorrow for both him and his family. There was even a part of her that felt bad for Emmett. She couldn't imagine being forced to spend the final moments of a loved one's life being shut out of it. It didn't explain why he'd done what he had, but she empathised with his heartbreak.

Tova had recovered, though she'd needed to have surgery on her bowel and had spent several weeks in hospital. Once she'd been released, however, she had used her ordeal to her advantage. Every time Macie turned on the television, Tova was on-screen, talking about what had happened to her on some daytime show or another. It had been announced that she was writing a book, and it had apparently already sold to a publisher for a ridiculous sum.

Tova had been in touch with Macie, asking her to not only reappear back on *Tova's Questions* but also to interview for the book. Macie didn't even have to think about it before she'd refused the offer.

The last thing she needed was more attention.

"It's getting cold," her mother called up to her again.

"Coming," she called back.

As she hurried down the stairs, her heart—Gregory's heart—picked up its pace. She put her hand to her chest and felt its steady thump through her fingers. *Thank you, Gregory.*

She hoped, whatever happened, he was with his God now.

# Acknowledgements

F irst of all, I'd like to thank Jacqueline Beard for putting up with my lateness! Sorry for my nagging email and thank you for making sure I caught my deadline. I really do appreciate that final read through.

As always, thanks to my long-time editor, Emmy Ellis. You know I both love and hate that highlight pen in equal measure. I wonder what 'pet' word I'll pick for the next book.

Thank you to Tammy Payne for your proofreading. I hope we caught all those sneaky typos! And thanks to Patrick O'Donnell for consulting with me on all of my crime books, and all the members of the Cops and Writer's group. The thought of only getting three questions in total filled me with horror—especially as I'm sure I've asked ten times that already!

Finally, thanks to you, the reader, for taking the time to read my books.

Until next time,

MK

# About the Author

M K Farrar had penned more than fifteen novels of psychological noir and crime fiction. A British author, she lives in the countryside with her three children and a menagerie of rescue pets.

When she's not writing—which isn't often—she balances out all the murder with baking and binge-watching shows on Netflix.

You can find out more about M K and grab a free book via her website, https://mkfarrar.com

She can also be emailed at mk@mkfarrar.com. She loves to hear from readers!

# Also by the Author

The Eye Thief
The Silent One
The Artisan
The Child Catcher
The Body Dealer
The Gathering Man

**Crime after Crime series, written with M A Comley**
Watching Over Me
Down to Sleep
If I Should Die

**Standalone Psychological Thrillers**
Some They Lie
On His Grave
Down to Sleep

Published by Warwick House Press

**Publisher's Note**

Printed in Great Britain
by Amazon